Sophie knew the hug was a mistake as soon as she'd done it.

She could smell the citrusy scent of his shower gel and feel the steady thud of his heart against her. And this surge of sheer attraction, tempting her to jam her mouth over his and let him lose himself in her, forget his pain for a while…

She dropped her hands and stepped back. "Sorry. I just thought you could do with a hug."

"I did. Thank you."

"I, um… I'd better go."

Panic skittered across his face. "Sophie, I know it's pushy of me to ask, but… I don't have a clue what to do with Sienna tomorrow. There's only so much storytelling and coloring we can do in a day."

"You could always do something messy," she suggested.

He looked horrified.

She frowned. "Didn't you do that sort of thing as a kid?"

"No. My mother didn't like messes."

Her thoughts must have shown on her face, because he said, "There's nothing wrong with liking a tidy house."

"And there's nothing wrong with a bit of a mess, either," she said. "It doesn't take that long to clear up."

And she left without finishing her coffee, and before she did anything really crazy—like sliding her arms round his neck and kissing him stupid.

Dear Reader,

I love Christmas, and I wanted to write a book about the healing power of Christmas. Hence we have Jamie, who's bereaved and blaming himself and won't let himself get close to anyone, and Sophie, who put her trust in the wrong man and ended up with a broken heart.

What brings them together are two seismic shifts in their lives—Sophie needs someone to buy out her partner's share of their business, and Jamie needs a temporary nanny for his young daughter, Sienna. They make a pact to help each other out, but they don't expect to fall in love with each other.

With the help of Father Christmas, banana penguins, a very special teddy bear and the gaudiest Christmas tree in the world, can Jamie, Sophie and Sienna get what they all want for Christmas and become a family?

I hope you enjoy their journey.

With love,

Kate Hardy

Christmas Bride for the Boss

Kate Hardy

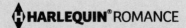

Recycling programs
for this product may
not exist in your area.

ISBN-13: 978-0-373-74463-3

Christmas Bride for the Boss

First North American Publication 2017

Copyright © 2017 by Pamela Brooks

Printed in U.S.A.

Kate Hardy has always loved books, and could read before she went to school. She discovered Harlequin books when she was twelve and decided *this* was what she wanted to do. When she isn't writing, Kate enjoys reading, cinema, ballroom dancing and the gym. You can contact her via her website: katehardy.com.

Books by Kate Hardy

Harlequin Romance

Summer at Villa Rosa

The Runaway Bride and the Billionaire

Billionaires of London

Billionaire, Boss...Bridegroom?
Holiday with the Best Man

Falling for Mr. December
Falling for the Secret Millionaire
Her Festive Doorstep Baby
His Shy Cinderella

Harlequin Medical Romance

Paddington Children's Hospital

Mommy, Nurse...Duchess?

Capturing the Single Dad's Heart
The Midwife's Pregnancy Miracle

Visit the Author Profile page
at Harlequin.com for more titles.

To Gay, my much-loved stepmom, who's living
proof that stepmothers are AWESOME.

CHAPTER ONE

'ALL RIGHT, MISS FIRTH. You have ten minutes to convince me why I should invest in your company.' Jamie Wallis leaned back in his chair, unsmiling, and looked at her.

Sophie caught her breath.

This was it.

The next ten minutes could change her entire life.

She needed to be more professional now than she'd ever been. And she really needed to ignore the fact that Jamie Wallis was one of the most beautiful men she'd ever met. The photographs she'd seen didn't do him justice. And Eva hadn't warned her that you could practically drown in his dark eyes.

Focus, she told herself. Because everyone's counting on you to get his backing. And you don't do relationships any more. Not since Joe. You finally learned your lesson: focus on your business.

'Thank you,' she said. 'I'm assuming you've gone through the accounts I sent you, so you'll already know our company's bottom line is solid.'

He inclined his head, still unsmiling. 'So why exactly are you asking me to invest in your company?'

She took a deep breath. 'Because as well as you owning several resorts, your company offers specialist holidays to travellers, so Plans & Planes—being a travel agency and event planning service—fits in very well with your business. Especially as we're introducing a new service which merges both sides of our company—something you don't offer at the moment.'

'Which is?' he asked.

'A planning service for people who want to get married abroad. We can organise everything from the wedding ceremony and reception through to the honeymoon, plus accommodation for the guests, and we'll deal with all the paperwork.' It had been her brainchild and she'd been so looking forward to developing the new service.

Until Eva had dropped her bombshell.

'And your approach to me has nothing to do with the fact that your former partner is my late wife's cousin?'

Sophie had expected that question and worked out her answer in advance. 'Eva suggested you as a potential investor, I admit. But I researched your company before I decided to approach you. I'm not looking for nepotism. I'm looking for someone who sees a good investment that fits in with their own business plans.'

'I see.' He steepled his fingers. 'What about the fact that Eva's leaving the company? How do I know that everything at Plans & Planes isn't going to take a massive nosedive without Eva at the helm?'

It was a fair question and Sophie wasn't going to take it personally. 'The impact of Eva's departure on the business is mainly financial.' The impact on her was another matter: Eva was Sophie's best friend as well as her business partner and she'd miss Eva hugely. 'Eva's deputy, Mara, has worked for us for the last three years and she's ready to step into Eva's shoes on the travel agency side,' she explained. 'Mara has the experience, the knowledge and the capability to take that part of the company forward. I'm staying to manage the event planning side and the new weddings abroad service, so there's continuity of management.'

He made a couple of notes. 'If the business is flourishing, why do you need an investor?'

'Because, as I'm sure you're aware, Eva is moving to New York with her fiancé.' Aidan had been headhunted by a top New York advertising agency and the opportunity was too good to turn down. 'So she needs me to buy out her half of the business.'

'And you have no savings you can use to buy her out, Miss Firth?'

She had, until two months ago. She took a deep breath. 'No.'

'Why?'

Telling him the truth would make it sound as if she was trying to manipulate him. Plus it was between Sophie, her brother and her sister-in-law. She wasn't going to break their confidence. 'Personal reasons,' she said.

'Won't your bank give you a loan?'

She winced inwardly, knowing how bad her answer was going to sound, but she wasn't going to lie. 'No.'

He raised an eyebrow. 'Because your financial management isn't good enough?'

'There's nothing wrong with my financial management,' she said patiently. 'The business is doing well.'

'Then why don't you have savings, Miss Firth?'

'Personal reasons,' she repeated.

'That, Miss Firth, is tantamount to telling an insurance company that you're a business-woman. It's too vague. They'll need to know precisely what business you're in so they can assess the risk.'

'I'm not asking you to insure me, Mr Wallis. I'm asking you to invest in the business.'

He gave her a cool, assessing look. 'Miss Firth, if you want me to invest in your company, you can't hide behind "personal reasons".'

Maybe she could tell him some of it. Broad brush rather than details. 'All right,' she said reluctantly. 'Since you ask, I lent my savings to someone I love very much.'

'Then surely you can ask that person to return the money, now you need it for yourself?'

'No.'

He frowned. 'Why not?'

Because the money had been spent, and her brother and sister-in-law were already under enough pressure. This was their fourth attempt at IVF, and she didn't want to make it any harder for them than it already was. 'I can't explain more without breaking a confidence.'

'So you'd rather see your business go under?'

'Of course not. We have four staff and a roster of reliable temps, and I want them to have job security.'

He shrugged. 'Then ask for the money back so you can buy out Eva's share of the business.'

They were at stalemate. Or maybe there was another way round this. 'Do you have siblings, Mr Wallis?' she asked, already knowing that he did but not knowing how close he was to them; not every family was as close as hers.

He inclined his head. 'Two.'

'If they needed you, would you hesitate to help?' she asked.

'Of course not.'

Just what she'd hoped he'd say. 'Then I can safely say you would've made the same decision I did, in those circumstances,' she said.

'Given that I don't know the circum—'

His mobile phone shrilled, cutting him off mid-word. He glanced at the screen, as if about to hit the button to decline the call, then frowned.

'I apologise, Miss Firth. I'm afraid I need to take this.'

From the expression on his face, this was definitely a private call, Sophie thought. 'Shall I wait…?' She indicated the reception area outside his office.

He looked grateful. 'Thank you.'

Sophie left Jamie's office, sat down on one of the chairs and closed her eyes.

The bank had already said no. It was pretty clear that Jamie Wallis, her plan B, was going to turn her down. So now she needed to work out a plan C.

Crowdsourcing? No. It'd make her look as if the business had run out of money. Which it hadn't.

Offering shares in the business to the rest of the team? But Mara was about to get married and the other three were saving up the deposit for a flat. None of them had any spare money, much less the ability to raise a loan to buy out part of Eva's share in Plans & Planes.

And Jamie's suggestion of asking Matt and Angie to return the money was completely out of the question. Her brother and sister-in-law had been eligible for one free cycle of IVF treatment; it hadn't worked and they'd already used up all their own savings and taken out a loan to pay for the next two cycles, which had also failed.

OK, so there were no guarantees that the fourth cycle would be the lucky one, and if it had been purely a business decision Sophie probably would have decided that the risk was too great. But this wasn't a business decision.

How could she possibly have stood by and watched their hearts break when she could do something to help? So she hadn't hesitated on offering to fund another cycle of treatment. She'd said it was a loan that Matt and Angie could repay whenever, but she'd always intended to quietly forget about the money. If the IVF worked and they had the baby they so desperately wanted, it would be the best repayment she could ask for.

'So let me get this straight,' Jamie said, scowling at the phone. 'You're telling me that Cindy broke her leg skiing yesterday, so she won't be able to walk, let alone work, for at least another two months. And you can't offer me a temporary replacement for her because the nanny who took over while she was on holiday is already on another assignment, and everyone else on your books is already either on an assignment and can't possibly be moved, or has gone down with a virus.'

'I'm afraid so, Mr Wallis. I know it sounds like a feeble excuse, but it's quite a nasty virus. It takes a couple of weeks to get over it. I'm so sorry,' Felicity, the agency manager, said.

'Effectively you're leaving me in the lurch.' Was there anyone in his staff he could ask to switch roles temporarily? He could hardly ask one of the resort team to move to London for two months, especially with Christmas coming up. There was nobody suitable in his London team, either. Those with children already had enough on their plates and he couldn't expect them to neglect their own children for Sienna. The ones without children didn't have the relevant experience. Short of asking his mother to help—and he knew from first-hand experience that his mother preferred to parent at a distance—Jamie knew he was stuck.

'I wish it wasn't the case, but I'm afraid the situation's completely out of my hands, Mr Wallis,' Felicity said.

He could try another agency, but he still wouldn't be able to guarantee having a new temporary nanny in place by the end of today—or that she'd be able to stay until Cindy was back at work. He didn't want to dump his daughter on a string of women she didn't know. Sienna needed continuity.

'How soon do you think you'll be able to get me a nanny to replace Cindy until her leg's healed?' he asked.

'I really don't know, Mr Wallis. It depends how quickly my staff recover. It might be a week, or it might be a fortnight.'

Although Jamie really wanted to shout

at Felicity in utter frustration, he knew that would be counter-productive. Fran had always said you caught more flies with honey. His late wife had always been more patient with people than he had; he found it hard to be charming in the face of sheer incompetence. 'This is going to be very difficult for me,' he said, resisting the urge to twist the guilt by reminding Felicity that he was a single father and didn't have anyone to take up the slack. 'But could you please call me as soon as someone's available?'

'Of course, Mr Wallis. Thank you for being so understanding.'

He forbore to comment, not trusting himself to stay polite.

And now he had a problem. A big one. An unspecified time—anything between a few days and a couple of months—without a nanny, and even when someone became available it might not be for the whole period that Cindy was away. He was in the middle of setting up a new resort, so he simply couldn't take the best part of the next few weeks off work to look after Sienna. He'd trusted the agency to deal with any situation like this, and they'd let him down. Badly.

What the hell was he going to do?

It was rare that he found himself in a situation where he wasn't in complete control, and he hated the feeling of being helpless.

Sophie Firth was sitting in the reception area outside his office. Right now, they were both in a mess. She needed someone to invest in her business quickly so she could afford to buy out her partner; and he needed a nanny for the next few weeks.

He could maybe help her—especially as Eva was his late wife's cousin and he ought to support his family—but right now he needed to focus on sorting out his immediate problem. He was going to have to turn her down.

He took a deep breath and went out to the reception area. 'Miss Firth, I'm sorry to have kept you waiting.'

'That's fine,' she said.

He raked a hand through his hair. 'I'm sorry—I can't help you right at this minute. Something's cropped up and I need to deal with it.'

Just as Sophie had expected. She needed Plan C. Disappointment still flooded through her. He wasn't even going to be honest and say he wasn't interested.

Something's cropped up.

And to think he'd called *her* on being vague.

Then again, there was something akin to desperation in his eyes—as if something had happened and he didn't have a clue how to deal with it. From the research she'd done on his company, she knew he was a shrewd businessman; his company had grown from strength to strength in the last few years, and even the death of his wife hadn't affected the business. What could have happened to throw him like this?

Before she could stop herself, the words came out. 'Are you all right?'

He looked at her in shock. 'How do you mean?'

'You look,' she said, 'as if someone just dropped something on you from a great height.'

'You could say that.' He sighed. 'It's my problem. I have to deal with it.'

But he sounded as if he didn't have the faintest clue where to start.

This was none of her business. She had enough of a problem herself. She should just walk away. Instead, she found herself asking, 'Can I get you a cup of tea or something?'

She cringed even as the words came out. It was his office, not hers. What she was saying was totally inappropriate.

But he smiled at her. The first real smile she'd seen from him. And it made her knees weak.

'That's kind,' he said.

'And inappropriate. Sorry.'

He shook his head. 'That's kind,' he repeated. 'But at the moment tea isn't going to help.' He looked at her. 'Given your business, you must know people in lots of different career areas. I don't suppose you know any nannies, do you?'

'Nannies?'

'That call just now was from the agency which supplies the nanny who looks after my daughter. Cindy—our nanny—broke her leg last week when she was on a skiing trip. And the agency has nobody available to stand in for her right now.'

So he needed childcare help?

Maybe she could turn this into a win-win situation.

'So I need someone to invest in Plans & Planes, and you need a nanny.'

He looked at her. 'Yes.'

'Maybe,' she said carefully, 'there's a solution that will work for us both. A business solution.'

'You know a nanny?'

'Not *exactly*.' She took a deep breath. 'What type of hours are we talking about?'

'Sienna's at nursery school five days a week, nine to four-thirty.'

Long hours for a little one, she thought. 'So your nanny takes her to nursery school, picks her up, and that's it?'

'And works evenings and weekends.'

So when did Jamie Wallis spend time with his daughter? she wondered.

More to the point, it made her own half-formed plan unworkable. Time management was one of her best skills, but even she couldn't cram an extra twenty-four hours into a day. 'Can that be negotiable?' she asked.

'How?'

What was the worst he could do? Say no. Which was pretty much what she thought he'd say anyway. She had nothing to lose—and potentially a lot to gain. And she wasn't afraid of hard work.

'I could be your temporary nanny,' she said, 'and you could invest in my business.'

He stared at her. 'You're a qualified nanny?'

'Not a qualified nanny,' she said. 'But my parents' next-door neighbours own a nursery school, and during sixth form I had a part-time job there—Wednesday afternoons, when I didn't have lessons, and two hours after school on the other weekdays. So I have experience of working with under-fives. Even if it was ten years ago. Plus I have a four-year-old niece and a two-year-old nephew, and I'm a very hands-on aunt.'

'Define "hands-on".'

'I see them every week. I babysit, so I do everything from playing to craft stuff and singing. I do bathtime, bedtime stories and the park.' She looked at him. 'I sometimes have to work with children as part of an event, so I—and all my staff—have an up-to-date Disclosure and Barring Service check certificate. And I'm happy to give you Anna's details so she can give you a reference from my time at the nursery school.'

A quid pro quo.

Sophie Firth wasn't a qualified nanny, but she was the next best thing.

'So you'd give up your job for the next two months?' he asked.

'No. That's why I asked about compromise,' she said. 'My business partner is leaving in six weeks' time. We need to reallocate all her work and recruit a new member of staff. Plus I already have a full diary. I can reallocate some of my work, and do the rest while Siena is at nursery school and at weekends.'

So he'd be with Sienna twenty-four-seven.

Just the two of them. His throat went dry at the idea. He couldn't do it. 'I need a nanny and weekends,' he said.

'I can do one day. Two halves, if that works better for you. But I need experienced staff, and recruitment takes time.'

This was starting to sound workable. 'I could lend you a couple of my staff to take off some of the pressure. Ones with experience in the travel industry and who've worked with—well, not events in the way you run them, but promotions. There must be a fair crossover in the skill sets involved.'

'There is,' she agreed.

'So if I lend you some staff, you'll do the full weekend?'

'Two half days or one full,' she repeated.

'I'm in the middle of negotiating a new resort. I can't take time off work right now.' That wasn't the only reason, but he wasn't discussing the rest of it with a total stranger. Even if she was potentially sorting out his huge headache.

'You said you had siblings. Can't they pitch in and help?'

'They live too far away.'

'What about your parents?'

Absolutely not. His parents had never been hands-on when he and his sisters had been tiny. They'd always been focused on the business. Until the next generation was old enough to have their lives organised—and that was one of the reasons why his sisters had moved to Cumbria and Cornwall respectively. Gwen Wallis had tried to run their lives in the same way she ran her business. Not wanting to explain that, he shook his head.

'I apologise if I've just trampled on a sore spot,' she said softly. 'That wasn't my intention.'

It sounded as if she thought his parents were elderly and frail, or had passed away. That wasn't the case but it was too complicated to put into words. 'It's fine,' he said. 'So you do weekends?'

'Two half days or one full,' she repeated.

He wasn't sure whether to be more exasperated or admiring. She wasn't budging. Then again, she was already making a big compromise—giving up a large chunk of her working week and meaning that she'd be running two jobs at the same time.

Admiring, he decided. Sophie Firth had a good work ethic—and she'd thought on her feet to come up with a solution that would benefit them both.

This was crisis management. *Good* crisis management. She'd seen the problem, come up with a solution and seen where the gaps were. It was the best proof she could have given him that she was good at her job, and investing in her business would be a sound decision on his part.

'Obviously I need to check out your references with the nursery school,' he said.

'And talk to Eva—you know her, and she's known me since our first day at university. She can give you a personal reference.' She took out her phone and handed it to him. 'Just so you can be sure I'm not calling her while you're otherwise occupied and priming her on what to say.'

He really liked how quick she was. The way she thought. If it wasn't for the fact that she was fighting for the survival of her own business, he'd be tempted to offer her a job as a project manager on his team.

'All right. If your references check out, you've got a deal.'

She'd done it. Sophie knew that Anna and Eva would give her a good reference.

But her conscience couldn't quite leave it there.

'Two caveats,' she said.

'Which are?'

'Firstly, you'll be strictly a sleeping partner

in Plans & Planes, and you don't interfere in the way I run things.'

He raised an eyebrow. 'What if I can see where you can make improvements to the business?'

'You can make suggestions, but you don't interfere,' she said. 'Though that's not the deal-breaker.'

He looked intrigued. 'What is?'

'Your daughter gets the final say.'

He frowned. 'How do you mean?'

'She meets me. We spend some time together. And then you ask her—and *not* in front of me—if she'd like me to look after her while her nanny gets better. If she says no, then it's a no.'

He nodded. 'That's fair. And it also tells me you're the right person for the job, because you're putting her needs first.'

But why wasn't *he*? Sophie wondered. Yes, he had a business to run—but it was much bigger than hers. He could delegate a lot of his work. Why didn't he take the time off to look after his daughter?

Given that she'd already made a gaffe about his parents, this wasn't something she could ask directly. She'd need to be tactful.

'Okay. I'll talk to Eva and your parents'

neighbour. Can you give me the numbers?' he asked.

He didn't know Eva's number? Well, maybe Fran—as Eva's cousin—would have been the one to stay in touch. 'You're probably best to call her at Plans & Planes.' She gave him the office number. 'Failing that, this is her mobile.'

He wrote the numbers down as she dictated them. 'Thank you.'

Anna Harris confirmed everything Sophie had told him.

'She worked for me during sixth form—two hours at the end of the school day, plus Wednesday afternoons. The kids loved her. I did try to persuade her to do her degree in early years education, but her heart was set on doing English.' Anna paused. 'I thought she was running her own business?'

'She is. She's, um, doing me a favour,' Jamie admitted.

'Ah. Typical Sophie. Of course you're right to check her out, but I have no hesitation in recommending her.'

'Thank you,' Jamie said.

It almost felt superfluous to check her out with Eva as well, but he wanted to be sure. For Sienna's sake. Because he did love his daughter, even if he kept himself at a distance. He wanted the best for her.

Only, the best meant *not* him.

He dialled Eva's number.

'Good morning. Plans & Planes, Mara speaking,' the woman on the other end of the phone said, sounding cheerful and welcoming.

Mara was Eva's second in command, according to Sophie. If her business acumen was as good as her phone manner, it boded well for the company, he thought. 'Good morning. May I speak to Eva?' Jamie asked.

'May I ask who's calling?'

'Jamie Wallis.'

'Oh!' For a second, Mara sounded flustered. Clearly she not only knew who he was, she also knew how important he could be to the future of the firm—and that Sophie was meant to be schmoozing him right now. 'I'll just put you through, Mr Wallis,' she said.

Eva answered, seconds later.

'How are you, Eva?' he asked.

'Fine, thanks, Jamie. And you?'

'Fine, fine.'

'Um, aren't you in a meeting with Sophie right now?' She sounded worried.

'Loo break,' he fibbed. Because explaining their deal would take too much time.

'Oh. Right.'

'Eva. Look, I know I haven't seen you for a while—'

'That's OK,' she cut in. 'Everyone understands.'

He mentally filled in the rest of it: how difficult things must have been since Fran died, and how it's harder to stay in touch with people who aren't in the immediate family circle. It was true, but he was guiltily aware that he often hid behind his circumstances.

'Thank you. I just wanted to ask you a couple of things,' he said. 'Would you mind?'

'Of course,' she said.

'You've known Sophie how long?'

'Eleven years. Since we met on the first day at university.'

'And you've been in business together for five years.'

'We'd still be in business together for the next fifty years, if Aidan hadn't been headhunted,' Eva said. 'But it's just not doable to run my half of the business from a different continent and a very different time zone, and it's not fair of me to dump all the work on Sophie and still expect to mop up half the profits.'

Good points, he thought. 'So you'd say Sophie was reliable and trustworthy?'

'Absolutely.' Eva's voice was firm with conviction.

And now the crunch question. 'And she's good with kids?'

'Yes. She babysits her niece and nephew all the time. Why?'

'Idle curiosity,' he fibbed.

But there was one little thing that was bothering him. He knew he was being a bit underhand, but he consoled himself that this was the quickest way to get the last bit of information he wanted. And wasn't all meant to be fair in love, war and business? 'And I've worked out for myself that she's kind-hearted. It was nice of her, wasn't it, to help her family with the money?' It was an educated guess; Sophie had only said she'd lent the money to someone she loved, but she'd also asked if he would help his siblings if they needed it. Which made him pretty sure she'd lent the money to one of her siblings.

'Yes, but that's Sophie all over—always thinking of others before herself,' Eva said. 'I really hope the IVF works for Matt and Angie this time.'

So he'd guessed right. She'd lent the money to one of her siblings and their partner. For a very personal reason: an expensive course of IVF treatment. And she'd refused to break their confidence by telling him what she'd done. Then again, if she *had* told him the truth, it would've looked as if she was trying to tug at his heartstrings and manipulate him. He liked the fact that she hadn't done that.

'Let's hope so,' he said. 'Thanks, Eva. Good luck in New York.'

'Thanks.' She paused. 'Jamie, I know I'm only an in-law, and not even a close one because I was Fran's cousin, but you're still family. Don't be a stranger.'

'Thanks.' Guilt flooded through him. He had been a stranger. Especially to Fran's family. Because how could he expect them to be rally round him, when he was the one responsible for all their pain—the one who was responsible for his wife's death? It would be like sprinkling salt over a wound. He couldn't do it. 'I'll talk to you soon,' he said, knowing it was a polite fiction and also knowing that Eva was well aware of the fact, but what else could he do?

Jamie walked back into the room and returned Sophie's phone. 'Thank you for your patience, Miss Firth. We have a deal.'

Yes. The business was safe, Eva would get the money she needed, and her staff had job security again. Mentally, Sophie punched the air. 'Thank you,' she said, trying to keep her voice businesslike.

'Though, actually, I probably didn't need to make those calls. I'm a reasonable judge of character.'

That's what she'd thought about herself. Dan and Joe had proved that to be a lie. She couldn't have got it any more wrong if she'd tried. 'I'm happier that you checked me out properly,' she said.

'OK. Do you drive?' he asked.

'Yes.'

'That makes life easier. I have a car that Cindy uses, so I'll put you on the insurance. Perhaps you could let my PA have a copy of your driving licence and let her know all the information that the insurer would need.'

'Sure. I have my licence with me.'

'Good. So are you able to meet Sienna this afternoon?'

If Sophie wanted to save her business, she didn't have much choice. She'd just have to move her meetings. 'What time do you want me to meet you at the nursery school?'

'It's probably better if I pick you up from your office and take you with me,' he said. 'Perhaps I could pick you up at half-past three, to give me time to brief you?'

'All right.'

'Thank you, Miss Firth. Or may I call you Sophie?'

'That rather depends on whether you expect me to curtsey and call you "sir",' she said dryly.

He smiled. 'Jamie will do.'

'Sophie.' She held out her hand. 'So, to recap, if Sienna likes me, then my side of the deal is that I'll be your temporary nanny until Cindy can come back to work. Your side is that you'll buy out Eva's share of my business, and lend me two staff while I'm nannying for you, to help with the transition.'

'Deal,' he said, and shook her outstretched hand.

Her skin actually tingled where he touched her. Which was so inappropriate—if this worked out, technically he would be her part-time employer and her part-time business partner. She couldn't afford to react to him like that. Worse still, he'd quickly masked an expression of surprise, so she had the feeling that he'd felt exactly the same.

This had the potential of being a complete and utter disaster. Especially with her track record in relationships, and in any case Jamie Wallis was a single father who really didn't have time for a relationship.

Maybe she should call off the deal.

But she didn't have a plan C and she needed him to buy out Eva's share of the firm. So she'd just have to ignore every bit of attraction she felt towards him and keep this strictly professional.

'One thing I should have asked you,' he said. 'Given that this means you'll be juggling your workload and it's going to take up more time in your day, will it be a problem with your partner?'

'I don't have a partner,' she said. 'And, just to make it clear, I'm not looking for one.' She knew that not all men were the same—her stepfather and her brothers were all wonderful—but she always seemed to pick Mr Wrong. Three years of dating Dan, and thinking that he was going to ask her to marry him when instead he'd dropped a bombshell; and then Joe, who'd lied to her from the outset and she'd felt disgusting and grubby when she'd learned the truth.

She wasn't going to put herself through all that again, falling in love with someone who would let her down and break her heart. After Joe, she'd promised herself that she'd keep all her relationships either business or strictly platonic. 'So I'll see you at half-past three,' she said. 'You have my mobile phone number in your file. If you could text me in the next couple of minutes, so I have your number, we can keep each other posted if anything crops up.'

'All right,' he said.

'And I'll see your PA with my driving licence on my way out.'

'Thank you, Miss F—Sophie,' he corrected himself. 'See you at half-past three.'

It looked as if he had a new nanny and a new business partner, Jamie thought as Sophie left his office. A bossy one who liked to run things her own way; but he thought part of that might be bluster. The fact she'd said that Sienna should make the final decision told him that she'd be fair and listen.

Sophie Firth intrigued him. She was the first woman to intrigue him since Fran. If he was honest with himself, she was the first woman to attract him since Fran—with those sincere brown eyes and a warmth that drew him—but he pushed the thought away. It would be too complicated to have any kind of relationship with her outside a purely professional one.

Plus, after what he'd done, he didn't deserve one.

This was going to be strictly business.

* * *

'So Jamie actually said yes?' Eva asked.

Sophie lifted both hands in a 'whoa there' sign. 'It all hinges on whether Sienna likes me.'

'Sienna?'

'He's got a nanny crisis. The deal is, if Sienna likes me, I'll be her temporary nanny until her real nanny's broken leg has healed. And in return he'll buy you out.'

Eva frowned. 'So what about Plans & Planes? Are you hiring a temp to replace you?'

'No. I'm borrowing two members of his team to help with the workload,' Sophie said. 'I'll be here when Sienna's at nursery, and I can catch up with paperwork in the evening.'

'Well, that explains why he asked me about you and kids when he called. I thought he just wanted to double-check that you were a safe bet in business,' Eva said thoughtfully.

'What did you tell him?' Sophie asked.

'That I've known you since our first day at uni, and if Aidan hadn't been headhunted we'd still be business partners when we're really old, and you have a niece and nephew that you see all the time,' Eva said.

Sophie relaxed. 'OK. Well, you certainly helped. I just have to hope that Sienna likes me—or I'll have to start dreaming up a plan C.'

'But you're going to be working stupid hours, if you're being a nanny on top of what you do here,' Eva said, looking worried.

Sophie shrugged. 'It's not for ever, just for a couple of months, maybe. I'll manage.'

She hoped.

'So, to save me putting my foot in it, what actually happened to your cousin?' she asked.

'They were on holiday, two years ago, and Fran fell ill,' Eva said. 'She died before they could fly her home. It was so sad. She was only thirty-three.'

'And that means Sienna was only two when it happened, so she'll only know her mum through photos and videos. Poor little mite,' Sophie said.

'Jamie was devastated. I'm not sure he's really recovered. Today was the first time I'd really spoken to him since the funeral,' Eva said.

'Didn't his family rally round?'

'One of his sisters lives in Cornwall and I think the other lives in Cumbria,' Eva said.

No wonder he'd said they were too far away.

'And he said his parents can't help, either,' Sophie said. 'So I'm guessing they're either too frail or they've passed away.'

'Oh, they could help, all right,' Eva said, 'but his mum would take over. Fran said Gwen was really overbearing and forever trying to organise their lives for them. The epitome of a difficult mother-in-law.'

'Ouch.' That might explain why Jamie's sisters had moved so far away from London, Sophie thought. And why Jamie seemed to keep himself at an emotional distance.

'Fran's mum is lovely, but Fran looked so much like her, I think it just brings back what he's lost every time Jamie sees her,' Eva said. 'Plus they live in Norfolk, so they're a bit too far away for him to be able to ask them for help.'

'Poor man,' Sophie said. Now she was beginning to see what made Jamie Wallis tick. And he had an even better excuse than she did for avoiding relationships: he was still a grieving widower, whereas she'd simply lost trust in her own judgement of people.

When Jamie left his office at half-past two, his PA raised an eyebrow as he passed her desk. 'Is everything all right?'

'Nanny crisis. I'm getting the potential temp to meet me at the nursery school,' he explained.

Her face softened. 'And how is Sienna?'

'Fine. And hopefully she'll get on with the temp.' If he kept referring to Sophie as 'the temp', hopefully that was how he'd come to see her. And he was absolutely not going to think about her caramel hair and how it would be lit with gold in the sunshine. For pity's sake. He didn't have *time* to think like that about anyone.

He called in at his house to pick up the file Cindy had left for the temporary nanny while she was on holiday, showing Sienna's routine, then drove to Plans & Planes. Sophie's office was very different from his own; the downstairs acted as the shop front for the travel agency, but when Mara showed him upstairs, where the event management side was based, he could see that the office was completely open plan, with two small rooms that he assumed were for client meetings.

Eva, who was sitting at one of the desks, came over and greeted him with a hug. 'You're a lifesaver, Jamie. Thanks.'

'Hopefully, Sophie's going to be a lifesaver for me, too,' he said.

'That all depends on whether Sienna likes me. It's the deal breaker,' Sophie reminded him as she joined them.

'Ready to go?' he asked.

'Ready.'

He handed her the file when she got into the car. 'Cindy put this together for when she was away. It's Sienna's routine plus a list of answers to the kind of questions she'd expect someone to ask.'

'That's useful. Thank you. I'll read it on the way to nursery school, if that's all right with you,' she said. 'And maybe you can answer any further questions I might have?'

'Sure.' He liked the fact that she was so businesslike.

Sophie's misgivings increased as she skim-read the file. 'Let me get this clear. You expect the nanny to get Sienna up in the mornings, then help her get her bathed and dressed and breakfasted?'

'And help her clean her teeth, then drop her at nursery school,' he finished.

'Why don't you take your daughter to nursery school yourself?'

'Because I have a business to run. I need to be in the office quite a while before she needs to be at nursery school.'

Sophie knew Jamie was a single father, but from what she could see the work-life balance just wasn't there. When did he get to spend quality time with his daughter? According to this file, he didn't even eat with her in the evenings. There was a menu of what looked like typical nursery food, which clearly she would be expected to cook. Did Sophie eat on her own, or with the nanny? Sophie's heart sank.

Fran had died two years ago, so surely Jamie should be smothering his daughter in cotton wool rather than using his work to avoid the little girl? It sounded more and more as if he was a cold workaholic who put his business first, second and third.

Sophie could remember what it felt like to be the daughter of a workaholic, one who'd missed every school performance and every parents' evening because he was always too busy. Her father had never had the chance to put things right because he'd died of a heart attack when she was ten. She was so aware of all the things they'd missed out on; even though her mother had remarried six years later and Sophie loved her stepfather dearly, she still missed her father and wished they'd had the chance to share things.

Maybe, she thought, she could change things for Sienna so the little girl didn't grow up with that same hole in her life, that same sense of loneliness and wondering secretly if something was wrong with her because her dad didn't spend time with her the way her friends' dads did. And, even if seeing Sienna reminded him of what he'd lost, at least Jamie still had his daughter.

Jamie Wallis didn't just need a nanny, he needed someone who could help him fix his relationship with his little girl.

And Sophie thought she might just be the one to do that.

CHAPTER TWO

WHEN JAMIE PULLED UP in the nursery school car park, Sophie asked, 'Should I stay here in the car? Because then it won't confuse anyone.'

'In case Sienna decides she doesn't want you to look after her? Good point.' He nodded. 'I'll be as quick as I can.'

He climbed out of the car, went over to the gate and spoke into the intercom, and then disappeared through the gate, shutting it behind him.

Sophie read through Cindy's file again while she was waiting for him to return with Sienna. The more she read, the more sure she was that things needed to change. Jamie was a workaholic, the way her own father had been, and he wasn't seeing anywhere near enough of his daughter—which wasn't good for either of them.

A movement caught her eye and she looked

up. She saw a little girl walking nicely down the path next to Jamie; obviously this must be Sienna. She was a pretty child, with a mop of curly blonde hair and her father's dark eyes.

She climbed out of the car and waited until Jamie and Sienna had reached her before crouching down so she was on the little girl's level. 'Hello. I'm Sophie,' she said. 'And you're Sienna, yes?'

The little girl nodded shyly.

'Sophie's going to spend the rest of the afternoon with us,' Jamie said, 'so you can get to know her a bit better and decide if you want her to look after you until Cindy's leg is mended.'

Again, there was a shy nod.

Better start as I mean to go on, Sophie thought. 'Would you like me to help you into the car seat?' she asked Sienna.

The little girl gave another nod, and Sophie's heart squeezed. Maybe Sienna was just a bit shy, particularly as Sophie was a stranger. She really hoped that Sienna wouldn't be this quiet once she'd got to know her; one of the joys of being an aunt was having a niece and nephew who chattered nineteen to the dozen to her and burst into song at the least provocation.

She opened the rear door, helped Sienna get

into the car, buckled her into the car seat and double checked it before climbing in next to her and buckling up her own seat belt.

'So what did you do today at nursery school?' Sophie asked.

'Painting,' Sienna said, her voice little more than a whisper.

'That's nice.' Sophie had always enjoyed the painting activities when she'd worked at Anna's nursery school. 'Did you bring any of your paintings home with you?'

Sienna shook her head.

Maybe the nursery school staff had kept the paintings for assessment purposes. Sophie tried another tack. 'Did the teachers read you any stories today?'

'Ye—es.' But Sienna wasn't forthcoming about what the story was, or what her favourite book was, the way Sophie's niece Hattie would be.

Then again, a car wasn't the easiest place to have a conversation with a small child. Sophie let the conversation lapse until they were back at Jamie's house. Then she helped Sienna out of the car, and waited for Jamie to unlock the front door.

'I'll give you a quick guided tour,' Jamie said. 'Obviously this is the hallway.' He took her through the downstairs, room by room.

'Living room, dining room, playroom, my office, downstairs cloakroom, kitchen.'

The house was beautiful, a large Edwardian villa with polished wooden floors, pale walls and windows that let in plenty of light; but it felt more like a show-house than a home. There were no pieces of artwork from nursery school held to the fridge by magnets or pinned to a cork board in the kitchen; there were no family photographs anywhere, either. And Sophie had never seen such a tidy playroom in her life. It made her wonder if Sienna was even allowed to touch her toys, or maybe there was a strict rule about only playing with one thing at a time.

This definitely wasn't a normal home. Even though her own father had put his job first, last and in between, her mother had made sure to give all three children her time and affection.

Then again, Sienna didn't have a mother to balance out her father's drive for work.

'I'll make us a drink,' Jamie said when they reached the kitchen. 'Coffee or tea?'

'Coffee would be lovely, thanks. Just milk, no sugar.'

'Would you prefer a cappuccino or a latte?'

'As long as it's coffee, I really don't mind. Whatever's easy,' she said.

'Fair enough.' He made two mugs of coffee via a very posh coffee machine and poured milk into a plastic beaker of milk for Sienna. 'I'll be in my office if you need me,' he said.

Obviously she and Sienna needed to spend time together so they could get to know each other, but this felt almost like an excuse for him to avoid the little girl. Or maybe she was being unfair to Jamie.

'Shall we go into the playroom?' she asked Sienna.

The little girl nodded.

In the playroom, Sienna agreed to do some drawing and colouring together. Sophie couldn't help noticing how the little girl coloured very carefully, making sure she stayed within the lines, and used pastel colours. So different from her exuberant niece Hattie, who always picked the brightest colours and wasn't in the slightest bit concerned if she coloured over the lines. The little girl reminded Sophie of herself as a child, desperate for her father's approval and never quite getting it.

'How about a story?' she asked.

Again, Sienna was quietly acquiescent.

'What's your favourite story that Daddy reads to you?' Sophie asked.

'Cindy always reads my bedtime story,' Sienna said.

'OK.' Sophie's sister-in-law Mandy had been very eloquent about the benefits of having a male role model reading to children, so her brother Will always read to Hattie and Sam at night. Maybe if she told Jamie, he might consider reading to Sienna. But, as her sole parent, why wasn't he doing that already?

Sophie read a couple of stories to Sienna, scooping the little girl onto her lap and persuading her to join in with some of the words. And when she made a tremendous pause before the last repetition of a refrain in one particular book, she was finally rewarded with a giggle from Sienna.

'What would you like for dinner tonight?' she asked when they'd finished the story.

'We always have chicken nuggets on Monday,' Sienna said.

Sophie remembered seeing the menu plan in Cindy's file. Just to check that her suspicions were correct, she asked, 'Does Daddy have chicken nuggets, too?'

'Daddy doesn't have dinner with me. He's usually still at work.'

'So Cindy has dinner with you?'

She nodded. 'In the kitchen.'

'Well, Daddy's home today, so he can eat with you and me. And we don't have to stick to eating chicken nuggets just because it's

Monday. Let's go and see what's in the fridge, shall we?'

Just as Sophie had hoped, Jamie clearly had either asked the temporary nanny to do a grocery shop the previous week or he had his groceries delivered. The fridge was half-full of fruit and vegetables; there were a couple of chicken breasts and a packet of minced beef. There were also a couple of supermarket ready-prepared meals, which told her that Jamie didn't bother cooking for himself in the evening and just shoved something into the microwave to heat through.

'Do you like spaghetti Bolognese?' she asked.

Sienna nodded.

'Good. That's what we'll have for dinner tonight. Daddy, too. Cindy's file says you have dinner at six?'

'Yes.'

'Great. You can help me cook dinner.'

Little girl's eyes were round. 'Can I? Really?'

Sophie's suspicions deepened. 'Do you cook with Cindy?'

'No.'

'Not even cupcakes or cookies?'

Sienna grimaced. 'They're messy.'

So who was the neat freak? Cindy the

nanny? Or was this an extreme reaction by Sienna, wanting to be super-neat and tidy so her father would approve of her? 'Mess is exactly what aprons are for. And vacuum cleaners,' Sophie said firmly. 'I make cupcakes with my niece Hattie all the time. She's the same age as you.'

Sienna looked shocked.

Oh, honestly. Sophie had to bite her tongue. Right at that moment she wanted to shake Jamie Wallis until his teeth rattled. The whole point about childhood was to have fun while you were growing up and learning about the world. And, yes, she could understand that not everyone was comfortable living in total chaos, but if Sienna made a mess she could also learn how to clear up again.

'We'll make cupcakes tomorrow afternoon,' she promised. 'With sprinkles.'

'Chocolate sprinkles?' Sophie asked hopefully.

'Absolutely yes.' She'd pick them up tomorrow, together with a few other things she enjoyed doing with Hattie and Sam. She smiled at Sienna. 'Right, I need you to do a very important job for me—can you show me where the pots and pans are?'

While she was directing Sienna to help her get the ingredients, she texted Jamie.

Dinner at six. You are eating with us in the kitchen. No arguments.

He ignored her text.

Well, fine. She wasn't daunted.

Just before she was going to serve up, she rang him. 'You have three minutes.'

'I'm in the middle of something.'

She didn't care. She'd already given him prior warning about when dinner would be ready. If he hadn't paid attention, that was his problem. 'I'm serving up now. Come and wash your hands for dinner.'

He hung up on her, and she wondered if she was going to have to go and drag him out of his study. But then she heard the door open and he strode into the kitchen.

Sienna beamed. 'Daddy, you're sitting here between me and Sophie. I laid the table. And I helped cook the bisgetti.'

'Spaghetti,' he corrected. 'Did you?' He gave Sophie a speaking look.

'She was a brilliant sous-chef, just like my niece Hattie,' she said.

Conversation during dinner was like pulling teeth. Jamie seemed to have no idea whatsoever how to talk to his daughter. Was he just hopeless with children in general, or was there something else going on here?

Sophie did the best she could to include both of them. Once they'd eaten, she said, 'It's bathtime, now, Sienna. Perhaps Daddy can do your bath and read you a bedtime story while I do the washing up.'

Bathtime.

Water.

Jamie had to dig his nails into his palms as a picture flashed into his head. Fran, her golden curls wet and plastered to her head. Her face so swollen and puffy, just like her throat had been inside, so no air could get through.

Fran, dead.

He'd avoided bathing his daughter ever since, leaving the job to Cindy. Sienna looked so much like Fran that he just couldn't handle seeing her with wet hair and getting those flashbacks, the dreams that had had him waking in tears for weeks after it had happened.

OK, so it had been two years and anyone would think he'd come to terms with it by now—he was overreacting. But he couldn't bear it. He just couldn't.

And Sophie really expected him to do bathtime?

Jamie looked horrified. 'Cindy—' he began.

'—isn't here. And you have a special question to ask Sienna which needs to be with just the two of you together,' she reminded him.

Oh, God. There was no way round this. He was just going to have to face his demons.

'Let's choose a story,' he said, desperately hoping that maybe if he dragged his feet a bit, he'd either be able to think of an excuse or Sienna might decide she didn't want a bath after all.

But it didn't work out that way.

He had to go through with it.

He made the bath as shallow as he possibly could.

'Cindy puts more water in—and more bubbles,' Sienna said.

'Well, we haven't got time tonight,' he said, hating himself for lying to his little girl but not wanting her to know about the nightmares in his head.

'And she washes my hair.'

No. Just no. 'Not tonight,' he said. 'And we need to talk about Sophie. Would you like her to be your nanny until Cindy's leg is mended?'

To his relief, it headed his daughter off the subject of her bath and hairwash.

'I like Sophie. She's funny. And she does all the special voices in a story,' Sienna said. 'And she let me help her cook bisgetti. I was her sushi.'

He couldn't help smiling at that. 'Sous-chef.'

'Can she stay? Please?'

'Yes,' he said. Even though Sophie Firth was pushing him into doing things he normally avoided. Because the alternative meant taking time off and doing everything for Sienna himself until the agency sent a replacement—which could take a couple of weeks.

He hauled his daughter out of the bath and dried her swiftly, before helping her into her pyjamas. 'Story,' he said. 'And then I need to talk to Sophie.'

Jamie had gone absolutely white when Sophie had suggested that he did Sienna's bedtime routine. What was the problem? she wondered. She was starting to think that there was more to it than Jamie being a cold workaholic. But what? She could ask him straight out, but she had the feeling he'd avoid the question. If Sienna agreed to let her stay, then maybe she'd have enough time to find out exactly what was going on—and help.

She'd just finished the washing up when he came downstairs.

'Well, you were a hit,' he said. 'I asked her, and she says she'd like you to stay until Cindy comes back.'

Though she noticed he didn't look too pleased about it.

'So I'm looking at my new sleeping partner, then?' she asked.

His pupils dilated slightly and she realised how her words could've been interpreted; she felt a tide of colour surge into her face. 'I mean my business partner who invests but lets me get on with running things and doesn't interfere,' she clarified.

'Business partner. And you're my new temporary nanny.'

'Right. I'm glad. Sienna's a lovely little girl. I'm going to enjoy looking after her. So I guess your solicitors need to talk to mine about the buyout, assuming you agreed with the figures in my proposal.'

'Uh-huh.' He paused. 'Plus I need to give you the car keys. Hang on a sec.' He fished a set of keys out of a drawer and handed them to her. 'And the spare key for the front door. I was thinking you might find it more convenient to stay here overnight in future. Cindy's staying at her boyfriend's flat until her leg mends, so you can use her suite—or the guest suite, if you'd prefer.'

Staying overnight? That hadn't been mentioned before. It wasn't part of their agreement. And she wasn't giving him another excuse to avoid his daughter. 'Ah, no,' she said. 'You'll be getting Sienna up in the mornings. Though I'll be here before you have to leave for work.'

He blinked. 'But Cindy—'

'—does things slightly differently than I would.'

'She's a trained nanny.'

Meaning that she was supposed to follow Cindy's instructions? Sophie wanted to rip that ridiculous file into little pieces and jump up and down on it. 'Well, I'm not,' she reminded him. 'As I said, I'll be here before you have to leave for work.'

'Right. And once you've dropped Sienna off, your day is your own until nursery school pick-up. I'll give you the code word, and I'll give the nursery school manager your details so she knows who you are,' he said. 'Would you mind if I took a photo of you for their records?'

'Sure.' She had something similar in place with Hattie's nursery school.

He took a photograph of her on his phone. 'Thank you.'

'And you make sure you're home in time to eat with us in the evenings.'

'I have to w—' he began.

'Of course you have to work—I realise you

have an empire to run.' She tried to keep the sarcasm out of her voice. 'But you're the boss, so you can choose where you work. It doesn't have to be in the office all the time. You have an Internet connection here.' She folded her arms and gave him a challenging look. 'So I want you here in time for dinner with us at six, and if you're late I'll make you eat cold, soggy, overcooked Brussels sprouts. And you won't be able to refuse because it'll be in front of Sienna.'

He looked utterly shocked. 'Oh, my God. Eva didn't tell me—'

'—that I was even bossier than your mother?' she finished.

His eyes widened. 'How do you know my mother's bossy?'

'What's sauce for the goose is most definitely sauce for the gander,' she said. 'You asked Eva about me—which meant I could ask Eva about you.'

'I think,' he said, 'maybe I should have tried a different agency for Cindy's temporary replacement.'

'Tough. You've already asked Sienna and she's made her decision.'

'I want you to go by Cindy's rules. Sienna needs structure and continuity.'

She needed love and laughter, too, Sophie

thought, but didn't say it. 'Let's try just a couple of tiny, tiny changes,' she said. 'Humour me. Spaghetti was all right tonight, wasn't it?'

'Well, yes,' he admitted.

'Good. Is there anything you really don't like to eat?'

He said nothing, but she could guess what he was thinking and grinned. 'Don't worry. I won't make you eat chicken nuggets or fish fingers with shaped potato products, peas and tomato ketchup. Hattie and Sam eat what Will and Mandy eat, so Sienna can eat what we eat. Plus, if she's involved in making dinner, she's more likely to eat it without a fuss.'

He frowned. 'How do you know?'

'My sister-in-law Mandy is a health visitor. I guess chatting to her, plus working at Anna's nursery school, means I've picked up a few things along the way.'

'I see. And I'm guessing you'll be the first to see the new baby, too.'

She looked at him, eyes narrowed. 'What new baby?'

'I know about the IVF,' he said.

She blew out a breath. 'Eva blabbed.'

'I made an educated guess and she filled in the gaps. Which I admit was probably underhand of me—I kind of let her think that you'd told me everything. But I like the fact you didn't try to manipulate me with a sob story.'

Sophie wasn't sure whether to be cross or relieved. 'So now you know the circumstances, do you agree you would've done the same for your siblings?'

'Of course I would.' He paused. 'Do they live near?'

'We all live in London. Not in each other's pockets, but no more than half an hour's Tube journey away from each other—and that includes Mum and Dad.'

He looked slightly wistful, and she guessed that maybe he missed his sisters. But asking him might be a question too far.

'Well, I guess I'll see you tomorrow,' he said.

'Sure. Though I have a couple of questions first.'

He looked wary. 'Which are?'

'Do you have a housekeeper?' she asked.

'A cleaner who comes in twice a week,' he confirmed. 'She does the ironing but not the laundry.'

'So laundry's part of my duties?' she checked.

'I guess I can handle that until Cindy's back,' he said.

'Fine. What about your grocery shopping?'

'I order online, and Cindy picks up any top-up things during the week.'

'I'll do the same. Obviously I'll make sure I have receipts for everything,' she said. 'And I'll give you a list of what I need you to order.'

He frowned. 'Aren't you using Cindy's menu?'

'Not unless you want to eat chicken nuggets,' she said sweetly. 'I thought we could have sticky salmon tomorrow. My sister-in-law Mandy has a gorgeous recipe, and Hattie and Sam absolutely love it. I can pick up the ingredients on the way to nursery school tomorrow afternoon.'

'OK. Anything else?'

'That's it for now.' She smiled. 'Goodnight, new business partner.'

'Goodnight, new business partner and temporary nanny.'

Sophie closed the front door behind her and headed for the small car parked on the gravel outside the house. There was a child's safety seat in the back, as she'd expected, so she'd be ready to take Sienna to nursery school tomorrow. She sat behind the steering wheel and closed her eyes for a moment. If anyone had told her first thing this morning that her life was going to be turned upside down for the next couple of months, she would never have believed it.

Right at that moment, she felt slightly daunted.

Sienna was so like the little girl that she herself had once been, desperate to please her dad and trying to be the perfect daughter. And it was heartbreaking, seeing the distance between Sienna and Jamie. They were all each other had. OK, so maybe this was none of her business; but on the other hand how could she just stand by and let the situation get worse, when she knew first-hand the sort of damage it could do?

Why did Jamie avoid his daughter? Did he doubt his ability as a father? Or was Eva right and he was so wrapped up in his grief that he couldn't think of anything else?

She had two months with them, maybe.

Would that be enough time to fix things?

This morning, Jamie had expected to have a short business meeting with Sophie Firth and politely turn down the opportunity of investing in her company.

And then he'd met her.

She was bright and she thought on her feet. She stood by her convictions and she wasn't afraid to say no. She'd practically glowed when she'd spoken about the new direction for her business. He'd liked her energy and warmth.

Maybe his nanny crisis was the answer for both of them.

Except now he was in a really weird situation: she was his business partner and sort of his employee at the same time.

He remembered the way she'd blushed when she'd called him her sleeping partner and then obviously realised how the phrase could be taken. And it felt as if his temperature had just spiked along with his pulse rate.

Oh, for pity's sake. He couldn't be attracted to her. It would be way too complicated. OK. This was simply a physical response due to abstinence, he reminded himself. He was not interested in what might make Sophie Firth blush all over.

And he wasn't going to let himself think about the fact that she was single. Available. Because he didn't have time for a relationship. He didn't want a relationship. He didn't *deserve* a relationship, not after what had happened to Fran. And no way was he letting himself lose control and fall for someone.

All the same, he found it hard to concentrate on his work for the rest of the evening. It unsettled him to realise that he'd spent more time with Sienna today than he had in weeks. He felt bad about the way he was avoiding his daughter, but every time he saw her she reminded him so much of Fran. The older she got, the more she looked like her mother, and his guilt crucified him every time he looked at her.

It had been two years.

Would it ever get any easier?

The next morning, Jamie found himself slightly flummoxed by having to get Sienna up, dressed and breakfasted. And his heart squeezed when he saw how grateful his daughter looked just to be spending time with him.

He really was making a mess of things. If Fran was here, she'd flay him alive.

But he simply didn't know what else to do. With business, he knew where he was. Being a single parent… It was better for Sienna that her nanny, who knew what she was doing, could look after her.

Or so he'd told himself for the last two years.

When Sophie rang the doorbell, he was shocked by how pleased he was to see her. Particularly because he thought it was more than just because she was rescuing him from his own fatherly ineptitude. And that would be a really bad idea.

'I'll see you later,' he said, kissed Sienna's cheek, and covered his confusion by rushing off to work.

Sophie noticed how Sienna's smile dimmed once her father had gone. OK. Today she'd look at what was happening, and how she could make small changes to bring Sienna and Jamie back together. Gradually, so he didn't realise what was happening and dig his heels in—because she'd already worked out that he was stubborn. But there was definitely more to it than him focusing on his work.

She took Sienna to nursery school, then headed to work at her own office. She picked up a couple of things for Sienna during her lunch break, reassured Eva and the rest of the team that everything was absolutely fine, then left the office early enough to drop by supermarket before picking Sienna up from nursery school.

'Daddy says I have to sit in the back,' Sienna said, her dark eyes wide with worry when she saw that Sophie had moved her car seat to the front passenger's seat.

'We're on my time, so we're on my rules,' Sophie reassured her with a smile. 'My niece

Hattie always sits in the front with me if I pick her up on my own. And we sing on the way. Did you do any singing at school today?'

Sienna nodded.

'Good. Then you can teach me the song on the way home,' Sophie declared, and strapped the little girl safely into the seat.

Sienna was shy at first, and Sophie deliberately got some of the words wrong, to make the little girl laugh and relax. And by the time Sophie parked the car, Sienna was singing at the top of her voice.

Back at Jamie's house, they unloaded the shopping. 'And I bought this for you,' Sophie said, handing Sienna a package wrapped in sparkly paper with a sparkly ribbon.

'But it's not my birthday,' Sienna said, her dark eyes wide.

'It's a Tuesday present, and you're going to be using it in, ooh, about five minutes,' Sophie said, 'so open it.'

Sienna was thrilled to discover a pink apron with white spots. 'It's beautiful! Thank you!' She hugged Sophie, who hugged her right back.

'My pleasure, sweetheart,' Sophie said. 'Right. Shall we make cupcakes?'

Once the cakes were in the oven, she texted Jamie.

Home by six or cold soggy Brussels sprouts. Your choice.

As she'd half expected, he didn't reply. But she was quite prepared to go through with her threat.

She and Sienna made the sticky salmon together, and prepared the rice and green vegetables. Sophie was pleased that the little girl started to chatter a bit more to her, talking about what she'd had for lunch and what her favourite things were.

Again, the little girl laid the kitchen table for three. She'd just finished when they heard the crunch of car tyres on gravel.

'Daddy's home!' Sienna rushed to the door to greet him.

Jamie looked a bit shell-shocked at the greeting, but to Sophie's relief he hugged the little girl.

'Daddy, the big hand on the clock is nearly at the top and the little hand is at six, so that means you have to wash your hands for dinner,' Sienna said, and Sophie had to hide a smile.

She clearly didn't hide it well enough, judging from the speaking look Jamie gave her. 'We've been practising telling the time,' she said. 'Sienna's very good. Maybe we can play "What's the Time, Mr Wolf?" after dinner.'

Was that panic she saw in his eyes?

But what was so scary about playing with a child? Especially when that child was his own daughter?

Deciding now wasn't the right time to tackle it, she served dinner. Jamie was careful to include Sienna in his compliments. But when the little girl was bringing a cupcake over to the table for her father, she tripped over her own feet and dropped the plate, which smashed on the tiles.

Sienna's mouth opened wide in shock, and then she burst into tears.

On instinct, Sophie scooped her up and held her close. 'It's OK, sweetie. It was an accident, and it's easily cleaned up.'

'But I made that one specially for Daddy,' Sienna sobbed. 'It had extra sprinkles.'

'We can put extra sprinkles on another one in a minute. Now, I want you to sit and cuddle Daddy for me so I know you're not going to cut yourself, and I'll clear up all the broken bits, OK?' Sophie asked.

Sienna's lower lip wobbled. 'I broke the plate.'

'It's all right. I promise it doesn't matter,' Sophie said, and glared at Jamie over the top of Sienna's head. Just when was he going to step in and reassure his daughter?

'It's fine, Sienna,' he said. And he did at least hold her while Sophie was clearing up, though he looked uncomfortable.

Sophie helped the little girl to add more sprinkles to another cupcake, and Jamie was suitably complimentary. But Sophie's temper was simmering just below boiling point. She agreed to do bathtime if he did the bedtime story, though she had to stop herself banging the pots and pans around while he read Sienna a story.

When she heard him come downstairs, she went into the hallway. 'Can we have a word? Your office?'

'Sure.'

She closed the door behind them. 'I'm keeping my voice low so Sienna doesn't hear me and start worrying. But I'm not your employee, so I don't have to be careful what I say in front of you, and I'm telling you now that I'd like to shake you until your teeth rattle.'

He winced. 'I'm sorry.'

'It's not me you should be apologising to, it's your daughter. Every child makes a mistake or drops things or breaks things. It's part of how they learn. It's not as if she *deliberately* threw that plate against a wall.'

He rubbed a hand across his eyes. 'I know.'

'She needed reassurance. From you, not me.' She put her hands on her hips and glared at him. 'And, for your information, I know first-hand what I'm talking about.' And even though she knew it was unfair to take out her frustration at her father's behaviour on Jamie, she could see that he was making exactly the same mistake—and that wasn't fair on Sienna. I'm speaking as someone who grew up desperate for her dad's attention, but he was always so busy at work that he didn't have time for his kids. I wanted to make sure I was the perfect daughter—I was his only daughter, so in my view I had to be better than Matt and Will, but I never felt as if I was good enough for him. He never made time for me. Is that how you want Sienna to grow up?'

'No. Of course not.' He looked shocked.

'I don't think you're a monster,' she said.

'No?' he asked dryly. 'Doesn't sound like it.'

'I think you're so caught up in your grief that you're forgetting you're not the only one who's hurting. And the people around you tiptoe round you instead of calling you on it.'

'Whereas you don't tiptoe.'

'Not any more, I don't.' She had, once. The people-pleasing from her early days had spilled into her teens and her early twenties. But her experiences with Dan and Joe had changed all that. She'd tried to be the perfect girlfriend, and she'd failed just as badly as when she'd tried to be the perfect daughter. And she'd got her heart broken twice in the process. 'I'm twenty-nine. Old enough and wise enough to call it as I see it.'

Jamie looked at her. There was something in her expression that said the tiptoeing round people wasn't just because of her dad—but now wasn't the right time to ask her.

'I'll make more effort,' he said.

'Good. Because she's a lovely little girl.'

Guilt squeezed round his heart like a vice. Except he wasn't sure he had a heart any more. Just a block of ice.

So he focused on business to push the emotion away, the way he always did, to put himself back in control of the situation.

'By the way, I asked my HR team to draw up a shortlist of the people in our team with experience in promotions as well as travel. They came up with a shortlist, and we have six people who'd be interested in the secondment. Perhaps you'd like to interview them tomorrow.'

She looked momentarily startled by his

change of topic, but then nodded. 'Thank you, I will. Do they all work at your office?'

'Yes.'

'Then it makes sense for me to come over to your office rather than call them all over to mine.'

He liked the way she thought. Economy of time. 'I'll make sure we keep a meeting room free for you tomorrow. Would half an hour each be enough?'

'If I can see their CVs beforehand, yes.'

'I'll email them over to you. And, Sophie? I *am* sorry about what happened tonight. I don't mean to be...' His throat closed on the words. *A bad father.* He knew he'd let Fran down and he was letting Sienna down. But he didn't know how to be any different.

She shrugged. 'Tomorrow's another day. Being a parent isn't easy. Draw a line under today and try again.'

Given her fierceness earlier, he was surprised that she was being so kind. And the way she'd phrased it... 'Are you sure you're not secretly a trained nanny?'

She smiled, then, and he was shocked to feel awareness pulsing through him. Sophie Firth had a beautiful mouth, and he actually found himself wondering what it would be like to kiss her.

Oh, for pity's sake.

This wasn't fair on either of them. He was really going to have to keep himself in check.

'I'm just an ordinary woman,' she said.

No, he thought, you're much more than that. And I can't let myself notice.

He needed to put a barrier between them; yet at the same time he found himself wanting to be with her. Learning what made her tick. Which was crazy. He couldn't do that.

'I'd better let you get on. I'll see you tomorrow,' he said.

'OK.'

She'd just got to the door when he said her name. She turned around and looked at him. And either his feelings were written all over his face or she'd picked it up in his voice, because she walked right back over to him.

'I think,' he said, 'I need help. With Sienna. Fixing all the stuff that…' He dragged in a breath. *All the stuff he was getting so badly wrong.* 'I don't have the right to ask you. We hardly know each other.'

'But I grew up with a workaholic dad. I can see things from Sienna's point of view— and from yours. So I'm the obvious person to ask,' she said.

His thoughts exactly.

'Plus I'm not your employee. So I'm not

going to tiptoe round you or be scared to tell you what I think.'

Could he?

Should he?

But her dark, dark eyes weren't full of pity. They were full of warmth. Of kindness. Of understanding. Part of him desperately wanted her help; part of him wanted to keep his distance and his self-control.

Though he knew he had to do the right thing, for his daughter's sake. Even if it cost him personally.

'Help me, Sophie,' he said softly. 'Please.'

She reached over his desk and squeezed his hands briefly. Again, it wasn't pity in her face but fellow feeling; and again, he felt that completely inappropriate leap of his libido.

'Yes,' she said.

CHAPTER THREE

THE NEXT MORNING, after dropping Sienna at nursery school, Sophie drove to Jamie's office rather than her own. He'd clearly briefed Karen, the head of his HR department, who showed her to the interview room and brought her coffee and a jug of water.

All the candidates on the shortlist were good and would fit in well with her team, but by the end of the interviews Sophie had two definite choices. She just needed to run them by Jamie first. She texted him.

Can I talk to you for five minutes re interviews?

He called her back immediately. 'Sure. Do you have time for lunch?'

'You actually take a lunch break?' she asked.

'Usually it's a sandwich at my desk,' he admitted. 'But it's probably a better idea to be away from the building if you want to discuss the interviews.'

'OK.'

'You don't usually have a lunch break, either, do you?' he asked.

'Busted. Same as you,' she admitted.

'Meet you in the lobby in five minutes,' he said.

She thanked Karen for her help, promised to give her a final answer in an hour's time, and went to meet Jamie in the lobby.

'There's a nice café round the corner,' he said.

'That sounds good.'

She let him shepherd her out to the café, where they ordered coffee and sandwiches, and found a quiet corner table.

'So how did it go?' he asked.

'They were all good candidates. But two of them stood out for me. I just wanted to run them by you to see what you thought.' She passed him the files.

'Good choice. That's who I would've picked,' he said.

'So it's a two-month secondment?'

'If that gives you enough time.'

'Just about. Thanks. Though we need to sort out salary payments and what have you.'

'Karen can advise you on the details,' he said.

'So that's number one ticked off the list,' she said. 'Now for number two.'

'Number two?'

'What we discussed last night.'

When he'd asked her to help him.

When he'd finally admitted that he was struggling to be a dad and hated that he was getting it so wrong. Jamie hadn't told her yet just why he found it so hard, but he would. In a few days. The more time he spent with her, the more he found himself trusting her. Eva was right about Sophie being utterly reliable.

But there was more to her than that. Something that he couldn't let himself think about. So he'd have to keep it strictly business, for his daughter's sake.

'Firstly,' she said, 'I think we need to rejig your routine so you always eat dinner with Sienna.'

'What if something really big crops up at the office—something that only I can deal with?' he asked.

'Something that big won't happen every month, let alone every day,' she said. 'OK. If there's a major crisis, then you call in advance and you explain it to her at her level.'

So he'd be eating dinner with Sienna every night. Seeing Fran's face in hers, and feeling the guilt twist in his gut. But he knew Sophie was right. For Sienna's sake, he needed to do this.

'Secondly,' she said, 'you need to do the bedtime story every night, because it's good for children to have a male role model as well as a female one when it comes to reading.'

'That sounds like something your sister-in-law would say,' he said.

'Got it in one,' she informed him cheerfully.

And how strange that the twinkle in her eye made his heart feel as if it had done a flip. Apart from the fact that that was anatomically impossible, it was totally inappropriate. Sophie was his business partner and temporary nanny. He shouldn't blur the boundaries and make this personal.

'Thirdly, from what I can make out, Sienna gets looked after by the nanny at weekends.'

'Yes.' He flapped a dismissive hand. 'Because I have to work.'

'Not every single hour of every single day, you don't. You need to learn to delegate,' she said. 'If you're going to build a bond with Sienna, you need to spend time with her—and that means doing things with her at weekends.'

He went cold. Getting really involved. Getting close to someone else he could lose with no warning. And he was like his own parents; he wasn't a natural at dealing with children. He didn't know how to relate to them. Plus he loathed all the tears, tantrums and screaming that seemed to go hand in hand with the playground. 'Please don't suggest I should take her to one of those play places.'

'Play places?' She looked baffled.

'You know the sort I mean—the ones kids get invited to for birthday parties. The places with a ball pit and slides and what feels like wall-to-wall screaming.' He'd always hated them and had persuaded Fran to take Sienna to them while he escaped gratefully to the office.

Sophie grinned. 'They're not *that* bad.'

'Yes, they are,' he said feelingly.

She looked at him, her dark eyes widening. 'Hang on. Are you telling me that Sienna never goes to birthday parties?'

'Of course she does.'

She folded her arms. 'But?'

'Fran used to take her. Cindy takes her now,' he admitted.

'OK. Well, doing things with her that you hate probably isn't the best idea. Scratch the play places, but there are other things you can do. You could start with the park on a Sunday morning—even if you just go for a walk and talk about what you see there, which dogs she likes and that sort of thing. Though Hattie and Sam love the swings and the slide, and if you time it right the play area in the park isn't usually that crowded.'

'Right.' He didn't believe a word of it.

'And it's Bonfire Night this weekend,' she said. 'I did a bit of research last night, and there are a few firework displays scheduled around here on Saturday night, including one at a local infants' school. I'll email you the details.'

'Bonfire Night.' Fran had loved fireworks. They'd had fireworks at their wedding. And Jamie had avoided them ever since Fran's death. Fireworks were the last thing he wanted to see.

'It'll be fun,' Sophie said.

No, it wouldn't. It would be hell.

'The school display is probably your best bet. It'll be small, they usually have quieter fireworks so the younger ones aren't scared by loud bangs, and there will be stalls with hot dogs and hot chocolate and glowies.'

'Glowies?' he asked, mystified.

She smiled. 'Necklaces, wands, tiaras and glowsticks. Kids of Sienna's age absolutely love them.'

'How do you know all this stuff?'

'Because I went to a firework display with Hattie last year. And it's worth giving in and buying everything on the stall that she likes, because there's no chance of losing Sienna for even a second in the crowd if she's lit up like a firework herself.'

'Got you,' he said. And maybe she had a point. Maybe it was time he faced his demons once and for all. Fireworks and Fran and guilt. 'All right.' He paused. 'Are you busy on Saturday night?'

'I'm supposed to be catching up with work. Though I guess I can move things round,' she said carefully.

It would be unfair of him to ask her, especially as he knew she was the kind of person who put herself out to help people and would find it hard to say no. But he couldn't face doing this all on his own. Being the single dad, seeing the pity and sympathy in people's eyes—pity he didn't want, and sympathy he didn't deserve. 'Would you come with us?' he asked. 'Please?'

'OK,' she said. Just as he'd known she would.

'I know I'm taking time out of things you'd want to do for your own business,' he said. 'And maybe I can help a bit with that.' Remembering what she'd insisted on as part of their agreement, he added swiftly, 'Not interfering. More like being a sounding board.' As she was kind of acting for him, where Sierra was concerned.

'A sounding board,' she said.

'Someone to bounce ideas off. Someone to listen. And you could even delegate some stuff to me.' He paused. 'Tell me about the Weddings Abroad thing.' Where business was concerned, he felt much more at home, He knew what he was doing. There were no emotions to mess things up.

'It came out of the event management,' she said. 'We plan all kinds of events, from corporate to personal—product launches, conferences, birthday parties and weddings. One of my brides was in tears, a fortnight before her wedding, because there were so many family arguments and everyone was being difficult and refusing to agree on anything. She said to me she wished she and her partner had decided to elope to Cuba instead, and actually asked me if I could cancel everything and arrange it.'

He smiled, guessing that she would've risen to the challenge. 'Did you?'

'No. I brokered a few agreements instead—a few compromises, so the bride got her happy day and the ones who were being difficult agreed to put their differences aside and be polite to each other for the wedding and the reception.'

Typical Sophie, he was beginning to realise. Fixing things quietly and sensibly, without a fuss.

Was that what she was doing with him and Sienna?

'But it made me think. Some people have difficult families, and others are maybe missing loved ones and would find it hard to have a traditional wedding in England without them. Having a wedding abroad would solve all those problems. So I looked into it, and found out what paperwork you need in each of a dozen different countries, how much time you need to allow for arrangements, and who to contact. Between us, Eva and I have the admin, the venues, cakes, flowers and dresses sorted.' She lifted a shoulder. 'It's just a shame that Eva's not going to be here to help launch the new service.'

'And you arrange the honeymoon as well?'

'And the hen night and stag night, if that's what my clients want.'

While she was talking about the project, Sophie was really glowing, Jamie thought. She was clearly one of these people who liked being able to wave a magic wand for people and make things better.

She was already making a difference to himself and Sienna—something he hadn't expected and was incredibly grateful for, even if at the same time it made him a bit antsy.

She glanced at her watch. 'Sorry. I tend to get a bit carried away when I talk about my pet project.'

'That's OK.' He'd enjoyed seeing her all animated. Though he couldn't help wondering why she was single. She was beautiful, she was nice, and she had an enormous heart. Why hadn't someone snapped her up years ago?

'I guess we ought to be getting back,' she said. 'But one last thing before we go— Cindy.'

'What about her?'

'If I were her,' she said carefully, 'I'd be worried sick about Sienna.'

'I've already spoken to Cindy. She knows Sienna's in good hands, her job is still there when she's ready to come back to it, and I'm still paying her full salary so she's not struggling financially.'

'That isn't the same as seeing Sienna for herself,' Sophie said. 'And I've been thinking about this from Sienna's point of view.

Please don't think I'm trying to trample on a sore spot, but her mum didn't come back from a holiday. And now her long-term nanny hasn't come back from a holiday. I think she needs to see Cindy for herself, so she knows it really is a broken leg and you're not trying to break bad news to her gently.'

That had never occurred to him, and it felt like a punch in the stomach. 'I...' He blew out a breath. 'Yes. You're right.'

'So would you mind talking to Cindy and asking her to call me, so I can arrange to take Sienna over to see her?'

How could he possibly say no to that? 'Sure.'

'Good.' She smiled at him. 'I'll see you this evening. We have fajitas for dinner tonight.'

He frowned. 'Fajitas. Are you sure Sienna—?'

'Yes. I won't make them overly spicy. They're one of Hattie's favourites, and she'll love them,' Sophie reassured him. 'I'll walk back to the office with you because I need to talk to Karen. Thank you for lunch.'

'Pleasure.' And, to his surprise, he found it was. He hadn't just been polite. It was the first time since Fran had died that he'd had lunch on his own with a woman who wasn't related to him or doing business with him.

This wasn't officially a date—but it wasn't entirely a business meeting, either.

And that evening, when Jamie went home, it actually felt like coming home. He found himself looking forward to Sienna running to greet him, to the scent of home-made food—to the sheer warmth of the place, something that had been missing for far too long. At the same time, it threw him; it made him feel less in control.

He washed his hands under Sienna's directions, then walked hand in hand with her into the kitchen, where Sophie was busy at the stove. 'What can I do to help?'

'Sit and enjoy,' Sophie said, putting the serving dishes in the middle of the table.

Without a word to Sophie, he helped Sienna load her tortilla with lightly spiced chicken, peppers, onion, salsa and guacamole. Sophie's smile said she'd noticed and approved.

It had been a long, long time since he'd found himself enjoying a family meal—and it was all thanks to Sophie. So, he thought, was the sparkle in his daughter's eyes.

Maybe he could do this.

Maybe he could be a dad.

Maybe he could be the family his daughter deserved.

'So how was your day?' he asked Sienna,

and was treated to a blow-by-blow account of her day at nursery and helping Sophie mix the spices for the chicken. It shocked him a little, because he'd never heard so many words from her in one go.

'And we're going to see Cindy on Saturday,' Sienna finished, beaming. 'We're going to make her a special card and a cake.'

Clearly Cindy had returned Sophie's call. 'That sounds good,' he said.

When they'd finished dinner, Sophie said, 'Bathtime now, Sienna.'

Dread coursed through him. Sophie had let him off the previous evening. Was she going to make him do bathtime tonight?

'And Daddy will need to wash your hair,' Sophie added.

He felt sick. But, short of telling her the truth about how he felt and why, he had no choice but to get on with it.

'Remember to put a facecloth over your eyes, Sienna, so you don't get any shampoo in them,' Sophie said.

He hadn't even considered that. What kind of rubbish father did that make him?

Gritting his teeth and trying not to let his tension show, for Sienna's sake, he took his daughter up to the bathroom. He ran a shallow bath—though at least tonight she didn't call him on it. Rinse, lather, rinse, lather, he told himself. And he managed it—thankfully because Sienna had a facecloth over her eyes she couldn't see the pain in his face when he looked at her wet curls. But he managed to dry her off, comb out the tangles and dry her hair. And when he'd finished the bedtime story, she wrapped her arms round his neck.

'Love you, Daddy.'

'Love you, too.' And he hoped she couldn't hear the crack in his voice.

'Thank you,' he said to Sophie when he'd settled Sienna to bed and come downstairs again.

'Just doing my job,' she said.

'Since you won't let me pay you for looking after her,' he said softly, 'you're doing me a favour rather than it being a job.'

'It's not about the money,' she said, flapping a dismissive hand. 'It's a quid pro quo. You need help; so do I. We're simply helping each other out.'

'All I've done is set the legal wheels in motion to buy out Eva's share.'

'And lent me two members of staff.'

'Karen tells me you're insisting on paying them, so that doesn't count.'

'It's fine,' she said.

'Actually, it's not. I feel as if I'm taking unfair advantage of you,' he countered.

She gave a hollow laugh. 'Trust me, you're not.'

That laugh alerted him. 'Sounds like experience talking.'

She looked away. 'It doesn't matter.'

'I think it does,' he said softly. 'Come and sit down. Talk to me.'

She shook her head. 'It's the proverbial hill of beans that doesn't matter.'

'*Casablanca*,' he said.

'Yes. Not that it was a Rick and Ilsa thing in my case,' she added dryly. 'Let's just say where business is concerned, I'm a good judge of character—but where my love life's concerned, I'm not so good.'

So who had taken advantage of her? he wondered. Whatever had happened had clearly hurt her deeply.

But she was already gathering her belongings. 'I'll see you tomorrow.'

'See you tomorrow,' he echoed.

And how strange that the light seemed to dim when she closed the door behind her.

The rest of the week followed a similar pattern for Sophie: picking up Sienna, dropping her at nursery, cramming in as much work as she could before nursery pick-up, then making dinner for the three of them. Jamie was clearly getting more used to the bedtime routine, doing bathtime and story time with a bit less reluctance, and Sophie loved the fact that he and Sienna were getting closer.

On Saturday morning, she'd agreed that Jamie could spend the morning in the office while she and Sienna went to see Cindy. They made a cake first thing and decorated it with pink sugar hearts, butterflies and sparkly sprinkles. Sienna had made a get well soon card, the night before, and Sophie had helped her to write the words inside.

Cindy buzzed them in through the intercom, and Sienna practically ran inside to hug the woman sitting in the chair with a cast on her leg and crutches propped up beside her. 'Cindy!'

'Oh, sweetie, I've missed you!' Cindy said, holding the little girl tightly.

'I missed you, too. Daddy said you broke your leg.'

'I fell over on my skis,' Cindy explained, 'and it's going to take a few weeks for my leg to get better. That's why the doctor put the big plaster on it.' She gestured to her cast.

'Sophie's looking after me until your leg's better,' Sienna said. 'And we made you a cake.'

Cindy blinked in surprise. 'You did cooking?'

'Me and Sophie cook tea every night, and Daddy eats it all up, every little bit.'

Cindy raised an eyebrow at Sophie. 'Really?'

'Really,' Sophie confirmed with a smile. 'Nice to meet you at last, Cindy.'

'And you, Sophie.' Cindy shook her hand.

'When you rang, you said there was a park nearby,' Sophie said. 'Maybe I could push you there in your wheelchair, so you can get some fresh air and Sienna can run around and go on the slide, and work up an appetite for a slice of that cake.' And it also meant she'd be able to talk to Cindy privately without Sienna overhearing.

'Sounds good,' Cindy said, clearly guessing exactly what Sophie meant.

'I made you a card, too,' Sienna said, shoving it into Cindy's hand.

'It's beautiful,' Cindy said when she opened it. 'A rainbow and a dog. That's lovely. And your writing's very neat.'

'Sophie helped me,' Sienna confided in a loud whisper. 'Sophie's really kind.'

Cindy gave Sophie an appraising look, and nodded. 'That's good. Shall we go to the park? You can help Sophie push my chair.'

'Yay!' Sienna said.

Once they were at the park and seated where they could see Sienna playing on the slide and the swings, Cindy turned to Sophie. 'I can already see the change in her. You're good for her. And I'm so glad you brought her over to see me. I was worrying about her having a string of temps.'

'Jamie was pretty insistent that he wanted continuity,' Sophie said. 'The agency let him down. Apparently everyone on their books was either already on an assignment or had gone down with that virus that's doing the rounds. Jamie was pretty angry about it.'

'So how do you know Mr Wallis, exactly?' Cindy asked.

'I co-own a business with Fran's cousin, Eva. Eva's fiancé has been headhunted, so she needs me to buy her out. I needed someone to invest, and Jamie needed a nanny,' Sophie explained. 'Although I'm not a qualified nanny, I had a part-time job in our neighbour's nursery school during sixth form. I have a niece who's the same age as Sienna and a nephew two years younger, and I'm a very hands-on aunt. Plus my sister-in-law's a health visitor, so I can ask her anything I need to. So this a kind of quid pro quo. I'm looking after Sienna, and Jamie's buying into my company.'

'I see,' Cindy said.

'I have to say, you're not what I was expecting,' Sophie said. 'Not after reading that file.'

Cindy groaned. 'The rules.'

'Which I'm guessing are Jamie's rather than yours.'

'I just wrote Sienna's routine down.' Cindy sighed. 'It's not what I want it to be. It just kind of evolved, and Mr Wallis is a bit set in his ways. But from the sound of things you're not sticking to it.'

'No, I'm not,' Sophie agreed. 'I guess the difference is I'm not actually working for him, so I can call things as I see them without any worry that I'm going to lose my job.'

'It's not so much losing my job I worry about,' Cindy said, 'as not being able to look after Sienna any more. I've looked after her since she was a baby.'

And she clearly loved the little girl dearly, Sophie thought. 'So you knew her mum, then. What was Fran like?'

'Lovely—a real dynamo, but she always made time for Sienna. Mr Wallis was different when she was around. He wasn't quite so much of a workaholic because she could always get him to stop and smell the roses.'

'Hang on. He still makes you call him Mr Wallis after four years?' Sophie checked.

'Fran was the one I saw most of,' Cindy

said, 'and Mr Wallis was always more formal with me. Though don't get me wrong. I have a lot of respect for him, He's a fair employer and he lets me take my holiday to suit me.' She gestured to her leg. 'And he's still paying me, even though I can't work.'

Money isn't everything, Sophie thought. 'Just he's totally buttoned up.'

'Losing your wife at such a young age is hard.'

'But it doesn't give you a good excuse to avoid your daughter and make your nanny look after her all the time,' Sophie said quietly.

'I think,' Cindy said, 'it's because Sienna's the spitting image of her mum and he finds it hard to cope. Every time he sees Sienna it must remind him of Fran and what he's lost, and he kind of buries himself in work to help him cope. Plus Fran once let it slip that he was pretty much brought up by nannies as well, in a house where children were meant to be seen and not heard.'

'So I'm also guessing he doesn't see much of Fran's family?'

'They live in Norfolk.'

'That's only a couple of hours' drive away. If he didn't want to make a weekend of it, he could still let her see her grandparents for the day.' She paused. 'Are you in contact with them?'

Cindy looked wary. 'Why?'

'Don't worry, I'm not going to march over to Jamie and blab,' Sophie said. 'My dad was a workaholic who died young, so I kind of know what it's like to be in Sienna's shoes. And I think she needs her extended family.'

'Agreed,' Cindy said.

'So I was thinking, sending them bits of Sienna's artwork and the odd photograph might be a way of starting to bridge the gap.'

'We're there already,' Cindy said. 'On my phone, I have addresses, phone numbers and email addresses—which I could accidentally copy to you while I update the grandmas on what's happening with Sienna.'

'Accidentally sounds perfect,' Sophie said with a smile. 'And that means they'll know to expect contact from me, too.'

'So you've actually got him eating dinner with Sienna?'

'And doing the bedtime story. He's done bathtime for the last three nights, too.'

'You,' Cindy said with a grin, 'are either a genius or you own a real magic wand.'

Sophie smiled. 'I'm just bossier than his mother.'

Cindy laughed. 'Now that I don't believe.

When you send Mrs Wallis photos and artwork, be prepared for a tide of advice and a bit of criticism in return.' She looked at Sophie. 'Though if you've achieved dinner, bath and bedtime story in a week, you might just be a match for her.'

'I'll keep you posted with how things go,' Sophie said. 'And we're going to a firework display tonight.'

'Just you and Sienna?'

'No. All three of us.'

'You definitely have a magic wand,' Cindy said. She smiled. 'Next you'll be telling me you've got him to do messy stuff.'

'That,' Sophie said, 'is an excellent idea. We'll start with glitter, I think.'

Cindy's smile widened. 'Now I know Sienna's in good hands.'

'She is,' Sophie promised.

That evening, they walked to the firework display at the local infants' school. Sienna was all wide-eyed and excited. 'We're seeing real fireworks, Daddy?'

'Yes, we are.' He masked his expression of pain almost instantly, but Sophie had seen it. What was so bad about fireworks? But now wasn't the time or the place to ask.

They wandered round the stalls together,

each holding one of Sienna's hands. At the stall selling glow-sticks, necklaces and wands, he bought one of everything for his daughter.

'You and Sophie need to have a necklace, too,' she insisted.

'These are on me,' Sophie said with a grin. She cracked the stick and curved it round, fixing it with the connector at the back of Jamie's neck.

'It's pink, just like mine!' Sienna said in delight.

He cracked the stick of Sophie's necklace and sorted out her connector, and Sophie was very aware of the way her skin tingled when his fingertips brushed against her. 'Yellow. You look as if your halo's slipped,' he murmured in her ear, and the tingle spread down her spine.

In another life…

But they were strictly business associates, she reminded herself.

'We need to take pictures to send to Cindy.' And to the grandmothers, she thought. Jamie duly crouched down to be on Sienna's level, and Sophie took a couple of shots on her camera.

'We need a picture with you, too,' Sienna said.

She crouched down on the other side of Sienna to take a photograph of the three of them together. And just for a moment they looked like a family…

But that wasn't part of the deal.

And even if she was in the market for a relationship—which she wasn't—Jamie Wallis wasn't Mr Right. It was way too complicated.

As if Jamie, too, was slightly discomfited by that picture, he shepherded them over to the food stalls and distracted Sienna with hot chocolate and a hot dog. And when the firework display started, he actually lifted Sienna onto his shoulders so she could see the display better.

Sophie could hear the oohs and ahhs of people around them as the fireworks burst into the sky; it was a magical display, but there was something even more magical going on right next to her, with Jamie finally starting to act like a father instead of a reserved guardian.

Sienna chatted all the way home, still holding both their hands, clearly thrilled about the fireworks.

'Will you stay for a coffee or a glass of wine?' Jamie asked.

'Coffee, please,' Sophie said, 'as I'm driving. Do you want me to make the coffee while you get Sienna into bed?'

'That'd be good. Thanks.'

Once she'd made the coffee, Sophie could hear him reading the bedtime story. His resonant and slightly posh voice reminded her of a Shakespearean actor she'd had a crush on for years. Sienna was clearly enjoying every second of it because Sophie could hear delighted giggles.

How much this house had changed in the last week.

Though they still had a long way to go.

She'd just sent the photo of Jamie and Sienna to Cindy when Jamie came into the living room. 'Thank you,' he said. 'Tonight was a lot easier than I thought it was going to be, because of you.'

'What was so difficult about going to a fireworks display?' she asked.

'Fran loved fireworks,' he said simply.

And she'd brought up all the memories. Brought back all the loss. Guilt flooded through her. 'I'm sorry. I wouldn't have pushed you to go if I'd known.'

'For Sienna's sake, I'm glad you did. Plus it was time I faced it. I can't keep depriving her of all the things Fran loved, just because it's hard for me.'

It amazed Sophie that he had such insight—

but she was glad for Sienna's sake that he could see it.

He raised his cup of coffee at her. 'And thank you for this, too.'

'No problem.'

'So I was wondering…how did you and Eva start the business?'

'Event planning and travel agencies aren't so far apart,' she said. 'I'd worked for an events company during the university holidays and they offered me a job when I graduated; it was the same for Eva with the travel agency side. And then I think we both got to the point where we realised we were stuck and we had next to no chance of getting promoted unless we moved to a different company. We were talking one night and realised how much the two businesses had in common. We'd both saved money, planning to buy a flat, but we put the money into the business instead. And I'm glad we did.' She paused. 'What about you?'

He lifted one shoulder in a half-shrug. 'My family's in the hotel trade, so it was always on the cards that I'd either work for them or set up on my own in a similar line of business. I was working for my parents when a former stately home came up for sale. There was a lot of land with it, including a wood, and it was the perfect place to develop as a resort offering activity holidays. I'd inherited money from my grandparents, so Fran and I talked about it and decided we'd go for it. We bought the property and got planning permission to build log cabins in the grounds. We built a pool and developed cycle trails and nature trails through the woods, and there's a lake where people can go fishing. And from there we developed a couple more.'

'I've stayed at one of your resorts,' Sophie said. 'We went for a hen weekend.'

'Not your cup of tea?' he asked.

'Going for a long walk in the woods in torrential rain is maybe not the most fun thing I've ever done,' she said. 'But I did appreciate your spa area afterwards.'

'I'm glad.' He smiled. 'That was Fran's idea. She said not everyone liked doing outdoor stuff and we needed something for rainy days as well, so we've got a roster of tutors and we run specialist creative courses—everything from photography and art to creative writing and crafts, cake decorating and pottery. And we listen to what our guests suggest, too. If there's a trend in their comments, that's something we know we need to add or change.'

'Again, not so far away from what we do at

Plans & Planes,' Sophie said. 'So how many resorts do you have now?'

'Four in England, one in Italy, one in the South of France where we offer a short course in perfume-making—that was one of Fran's last ideas. And we were thinking of developing one in the Caribbean, but...' He tailed off and shook his head. 'Not after Fran died. I couldn't bear to go back.'

She could see the pain in his eyes. 'I'm sorry,' she said. 'I shouldn't have asked. This must be difficult for you.'

He grimaced. 'I'm being maudlin. I'll shut up.'

'Maybe,' she said, 'talking about her will help.'

'Nothing helps,' he said, and she could see the loneliness in his face.

How could she just let him sit there and suffer?

So she walked over to the sofa, sat down beside him and wrapped her arms round him.

She knew the hug was a mistake as soon as she'd done it. She could smell the citrusy scent of his shower gel and feel the steady thud of his heart against her. And this surge of sheer attraction, tempting her to jam her mouth over his and let him lose himself in her, forget his pain for a while...

This was insane.

It had to stop.

Now.

She dropped her hands pulled away. 'Sorry. I overstepped the boundaries. I just thought you could do with a hug.'

'I did. Thank you,' he said.

Though she noticed that his pupils were huge. And she had a nasty feeling that her own were in a similar state. She couldn't even put it down to low lighting because she'd left the overhead light on. 'I, um, I'd better get going.'

'Thank you for today,' he said. 'For everything you've done. I appreciate it.'

'No problem. I'll see you Monday.'

Panic skittered across his face. 'Sophie, I know it's pushy of me to ask, but... I don't have a clue what to do with Sienna tomorrow. There's only so much story-telling and colouring we can do in a day.'

'You could always do something messy,' she suggested.

'Messy?'

'Glitter. Glue. Paint.'

He looked horrified.

She frowned. 'Didn't you do that sort of thing as a kid?'

'No. My mother didn't like mess.'

And you either followed in your parents' footsteps or you rebelled. From what she'd read in Cindy's file, clearly Jamie had chosen to walk the same path as his mother.

Her thoughts must have shown on her face, because he said, 'There's nothing wrong with liking a tidy house.' She could even hear the slight defensiveness in his tone.

'And there's nothing wrong with a bit of mess, either,' she said. 'It doesn't take that long to clear up.' She'd call into the shops on the way here tomorrow, to get the art supplies she knew he didn't have. 'I'll see you tomorrow at eleven.'

And she left without finishing her coffee, and before she did anything really crazy— like sliding her arms round his neck and kissing him stupid.

Jamie hadn't felt this mixed up in a long time. Since Sophie had put her arms round him like that, it felt as if part of him had been locked away and the key was rusty but starting to turn in the lock.

How close he'd been to leaning forward and kissing her. Finding out if that perfect Cupid's bow of a mouth tasted as sweet as it looked. If she'd kept her arms round him for one more second, he knew he would've wrapped his own arms round her in return and kissed her until they were both dizzy.

It was just as well she'd pulled away.

He didn't want to feel, to lay himself open to risking the devastation of losing someone close again, the way he'd lost Fran. Plus his guilt told him he didn't deserve that kind of closeness.

But part of him longed to see the daylight again. To see the world in full colour.

And when Sophie Firth had wrapped her arms around him, the world had felt bright again. Real. Warm. *Living.*

He was going to have to be really, really careful. Take cold showers. Mentally tattoo a note on his hand to keep his distance. For all their sakes.

CHAPTER FOUR

ON SUNDAY MORNING, Sophie visited a nearby toyshop to buy art supplies, then drove to Jamie's house.

'Sunday morning is art morning in my niece Hattie's house,' she announced to Sienna. 'So I thought we could do the same. I brought us some paint, paper, brushes and stuff.'

The little girl looked thrilled. 'Really?'

'Really. I thought we could make firework pictures. I used to do this when I worked at the nursery school, and it's really fun.' She smiled at Jamie. 'While Sienna and I set up the playroom, your job is to fish some cardboard tubes out of the recycling bin, Jamie.'

'But won't they be—well, all messy?' he asked.

Not as messy as what she planned to make him do, she thought, hiding a smile. 'It's the recycling bin,' she reminded him. 'They're clean when they go in and so are the tins and plastic.'

She shepherded Sienna into the playroom, fished a large square of plastic sheeting out of her bag and spread it over the table to protect it, then got Sienna to put on a long-sleeved apron. 'Now it doesn't matter if we get a bit messy—that's what aprons are for,' she said. She put a large sheet of paper on the table in front of Sienna. 'Would you like to choose two colours of paint?'

'Pink,' Sienna said immediately—just as Sophie's niece would have done, and Sophie had to hide her grin. 'And yellow.'

Sophie squeezed pink and yellow paint from the bottles onto paper plates.

'And now for the clever bit,' she said when Jamie returned with the cardboard tubes. 'Where are the scissors, Sienna?'

'In the drawer.' Sienna gestured to the cupboard where her toys and colouring pencils were kept.

'Thank you.' Sophie retrieved the scissors, made cuts halfway down the first tube, spaced a centimetre apart, then spread the fronds out to make a kind of fan. 'So what we do now is dip the cardboard in the paint, press it on the paper and lift it up again.'

Sienna followed her directions. 'Oh—it looks just like the fireworks in the sky last night!'

'I think Daddy should do some, too,' Sophie said, unable to resist.

'Ah—no. I need to get some work done,' he said.

'You can spare us ten minutes.' No way was she letting him wriggle out of this. 'Would you like to use the same paint, Jamie, or a different colour?'

'The same paint's fine,' he said, giving her a speaking look, but to her relief he knelt down by Sienna's table and duly made some firework patterns on another piece of paper.

'And we can use different sized fans to make different sized fireworks,' she said, cutting some more of the cardboard rolls.

Sienna was delighted, and even more thrilled when Sophie produced glitter from the bag.

'This is how we make the picture sparkle,' Sophie said. Out of the corner of her eye, she could see Jamie flinching at the idea of glitter everywhere. She managed to get his attention, then mouthed, 'That's what a vacuum cleaner's for.'

And to his credit he made more pictures with Sienna, chatting to her about her favourite fireworks from last night and even sprinkling glitter on top of the paint with her. Sophie didn't say a word, but she was thrilled that he wasn't using his normal excuse of work to rush away. He was actually spending quality time with this daughter.

They went from making firework pictures to painting with brushes, and Jamie delighted Sienna by painting the outline of a cat for her to paint in. 'I didn't know you could draw kitties, Daddy!'

He looked as if he'd just surprised himself, too. Sophie sat back on her haunches, watching them with a smile. It was lovely to see Jamie really interacting with Sienna, the way her brother always had with Hattie and Sam, especially as she knew from talking to Cindy that he was way out of his comfort zone with messy play. And when Sienna— with paint and glitter on her hands—leaned across the table, saying, 'I love you, Daddy,' and left paint and glitter smeared all over his white shirt, Sophie held her breath. Would this be his breaking point? A man who liked order and control would find this particularly hard to deal with.

But, instead of being snippy about the mess she'd made of his shirt, he simply said, 'I love you, too, Sienna,' and kissed her.

And right at that moment, Sophie thought, I could love you, too...

She shook herself.

That wasn't going to happen.

She was rubbish at relationships, and Jamie's life was already complicated enough without adding her into the mix.

'I need to go,' she said when Sienna had had her fill of painting. 'I'll clear up all the art stuff first.'

'Don't worry about it. I'll clear up,' Jamie said, surprising her. 'Stay for lunch. Even if it is only going to be cheese on toast.'

She blinked. 'You're offering to cook for me?'

'I can cook,' he said.

She thought back to the supermarket ready meals she'd seen in the fridge. 'I'm not sure I believe you.'

'Here's the deal,' he said. 'If I burn lunch, I clear up. If I don't, you clear up.' He mouthed, 'And you clean the paint out of my shirt.'

'Deal,' she said. 'Sienna and I will lay the table while you make the cheese on toast.'

And it was perfect.

'Now do you believe me?' he asked with a grin.

She raised an eyebrow. 'Strictly speaking, cheese on toast isn't actually cooking. It's just putting bread and cheese under the grill.'

'It still counts,' he insisted. 'Doesn't it, Sienna?'

The little girl nodded. 'But only if I make it with you next time.'

'I think you might have a negotiator in the making there,' Sophie said.

After lunch, she cleared away. 'I need to go now,' she said with a smile. 'But it's a nice day. Maybe you could both go to the park.' When panic skittered across Jamie's face, she said, 'Sienna, do you want to go upstairs and find a nice warm jumper?' Once the little girl was out of earshot, she said to Jamie, 'It'll be fine. You've got this.'

'How do you know I can do it?'

'Because I do,' she said. 'This is like dropping you into a pool full of cetapods and expecting you to swim. You won't know if the cetapods are whales or sharks until you swim up to them. But when you do, you'll realise they're all whales.'

'What if they turn out to be sharks?' he asked.

'Then you call me, and I'll come and fish you out before the sharks eat you. Now go and change your shirt so I can get the paint out of that one.'

'Bossy,' he said, but he did what she'd asked.

Even though Sophie was supposed to be working at home, she spent most of the afternoon thinking about Jamie and wondering how he was coping. But when he didn't call, she knew he didn't need her.

Which was meant to be a good thing.

Though it left her feeling slightly melancholy—and then cross with herself for being so ridiculous. Jamie Wallis was off limits. And the unexpected feelings she'd started having towards him were simply because she was spending so much time with him. Propinquity. She knew he thought of her solely as Sienna's temporary nanny and his business partner.

'So don't even start to begin hoping that things might be different,' she told herself sharply. 'Because they're not. You keep it professional. No emotions.'

In the park, Jamie couldn't stop thinking about Sophie. What was it she'd said? Go for a walk, talk about what you see, ask Sienna about her favourite dogs.

It was the first time he'd ever taken Sienna to the park on his own; before Fran's death, they'd gone as a family, and afterwards he'd left it to Cindy, because trying to pretend that everything was normal had just been unbearable.

But this… Since Sophie had pushed him

out of his comfort zone this morning, he was going to give this a try. He walked round the park with Sienna, holding her hand and letting her chat to him. And then, when he could see that the play area wasn't too crowded and hear that the shrieking was at bearable level, he pushed her on the swings and even went down the big slide with her. He smiled nicely at the other families in the play area and tried to ignore the ache of missing Fran.

And then he felt a flood of guilt when he realised that the figure next to him in his head wasn't Fran: she was Sophie. Which wasn't anywhere near their arrangement. He needed to forget the idea of this right now, because he wasn't going to get a second chance to mess up.

But the thought wouldn't quite shift.

Whenever his skin had accidentally made contact with hers, he'd noticed a faint blush on her cheeks, or her pupils had grown larger. He had a feeling that she was just as aware of him as he was of her.

What if…?

A tingle ran down his spine and he shook himself mentally. No. It had to stay strictly business between them. And he needed to get his self-control back. Fast.

* * *

On Monday morning, when Sophie walked into the kitchen, she handed Jamie's clean but unironed shirt back to him. 'It was washable paint. Easy-peasy.'

'Thank you,' he said, and his slightly shamefaced expression told her that he knew he'd made an idiot of himself over the messiness issue.

'So how were the sharks?' she asked.

'You were right. They were whales,' he told her.

She smiled. 'Good. Now go to work. Sienna and I have stuff to do.'

Funny how easily she'd slipped into a routine. It felt second nature to take Sienna to nursery school before she went to the office, then to pick her up and cook dinner together, to read together and sing and play.

This felt like being part of a family.

Like the life she'd expected to have with Daniel, until he'd dropped his bombshell. Like the life she'd thought to build with Joe—until she'd learned the truth about him. So what was to say this would be third time lucky? With her track record, it'd be third time unlucky. And there was Sienna to consider. The little girl had had more than enough upheaval in her short life. She didn't need the prospect of more heartbreak.

This was temporary, Sophie reminded herself. And she loved her job. She was happy concentrating on her career and looking forward to going ahead with the new strand to the business, organising weddings abroad.

But, as every day passed, she found herself growing closer and closer to both Sienna and her father. Even though she tried to keep a tiny bit of distance in there, particularly with Jamie, it felt as if it was melting away by the second.

And when on Friday evening he was struggling to come up with ideas of things to do with Sienna at the weekend, how could she refuse to help him?

'The aquarium's always a hit with Hattie and Sam,' she said. 'They love watching the fish and going through the tunnel to see the sharks. Oh, and the penguins. They're Hattie's favourite.'

'Would you come with us tomorrow afternoon?' he asked.

She ought to say no. Keep the distance between them. But he needed her help and she couldn't just turn away. That wasn't who she was. Besides, she could always get up a couple of hours early to catch up with her own work. Thanks to Jamie lending her two really talented members of his team, everything was going just fine at Plans & Planes. 'Sure. Provided I get to look at the jellyfish and the sea horses—they're my favourites.'

'Deal,' he said. 'And I'm paying for your ticket, as I asked you to join us.'

'Only if I buy us dinner. And that's non-negotiable.'

'All right. Thank you,' he said.

'I'll meet you at the front door—say two o'clock?'

'That'd be perfect,' he said.

Outside the aquarium, Sienna greeted Sophie with a squeal and a hug. Jamie's greeting was rather more restrained, but even so his smile made Sophie's heart feel as if it had just done a backward somersault.

She was really going to have to keep a tight rein on herself. He's off limits, she reminded herself. But it felt as if part of her was standing there with her fingers stuck in her ears, saying, 'La-la-la—I can't hear you.'

Jamie had already printed out their tickets at home, to save them having to queue up, and they headed for the penguin zone. He'd clearly read up about the creatures, because he said to Sienna, 'These ones are called Gentoo penguins. And their black and white colouring is camouflage for them.'

'What's camoo…?' Sienna frowned.

'Camouflage,' he repeated carefully. 'It means a special colouring so they look like their surroundings.'

'But water's blue, Daddy. Why aren't they blue, too?'

He smiled. 'It's all to do with how light looks under water. The water looks black and the sunlight looks white. So the camouflage means the penguins look like water and sunlight to any big killer whales that might come along and want to eat them.'

Sienna shivered. 'I don't like whales. I like penguins.'

'There aren't any killer whales here,' Sophie promised her. 'But not all whales eat penguins. Some whales just eat fish, like the minke whales.'

'What's a minke whale?' Sienna asked.

'A very pretty black and white whale. I went to Iceland last summer and I saw minke whales playing in the sea, and they're beautiful.' Sophie grabbed her phone and scrolled through it until she found a photograph. 'Look. I was at the front of the boat and I saw one jump all the way out of the sea and I took his picture—isn't he beautiful?'

Sophie stared at the picture, her eyes round with amazement. 'He jumped all the way out of the sea?'

'Right in front of my eyes. It was amazing,' Sophie confirmed.

'Iceland. Would that have been a research trip for your Weddings Abroad project?' Jamie asked, looking interested.

She nodded. 'I saw half a dozen brides while I was out there. Apparently it's very popular to have the wedding ceremony one day, then go out to do photographs the next day, either on one of the black sand beaches or at one of the waterfalls. Can you imagine how amazing it is to have rainbows in your wedding photos?'

'I like rainbows,' Sienna said.

'They're my favourite, too,' Sophie said. 'Rainbows and the Northern Lights. Though obviously you don't see the Northern Lights in the summer, because you've got the midnight sun. And that's beautiful, too.'

'Are you going to get married, like Cindy and Jack are?' Sienna asked.

She'd thought so. Twice. And how very wrong she'd been. 'Maybe one day,' she said.

'Cindy said I could be her bridesmaid. Can I be your bridesmaid, too?'

'We'll see, sweetie,' Sophie said gently. 'That might be a long time in the future.'

* * *

Jamie saw a flicker of sadness in Sophie's eyes. That, plus what she'd said to him a while back about not having good judgement where her love life was concerned, made him sure that someone had let her down very badly. And that brief moment of sadness made him want to give her a hug.

Then again, that probably wasn't a good idea. When she'd given him a hug, it had made all sorts of feelings start bubbling up—feelings he couldn't afford to have. In his experience, love meant loss—something he never wanted to risk again. And he was going to have to make a real effort not to let himself be drawn to her.

She'd sounded wistful when she'd talked about rainbows in wedding photos. Was that what she'd wanted? But it would hardly be tactful to ask. And he needed to head his daughter off before *she* asked. 'Hey, Sienna, do you know what penguins' wings are called?' he asked.

'They don't have wings. Penguins can't fly,' Sienna said.

'Ah, but they do have wings,' he said with a smile. 'Instead of using them to fly, they use their wings to help them swim.'

Swim. He pushed thoughts of Fran away.

Nobody was swimming here apart from the creatures who lived in the water. And there wasn't any coral that he could see.

'I know—flippers!' Sienna said.

'That's right.'

They watched the penguins sliding down the ice on their bellies and dive into the water.

'They're so clever, Daddy,' Sienna said, her nose practically pressed against the glass as she watched them.

'They certainly are. Did you know that Gentoo penguins make their nests out of pebbles rather than sticks?'

'I didn't know that, either,' Sophie said. 'I'll remember to tell Hattie that.'

They headed through the shark tunnel, and Sienna was fascinated by the sight of the sharks swimming beneath their feet.

'Did you know some sharks can lose thirty thousand teeth in their lifetime?' Sophie asked.

And Jamie thought, Sophie's full of the kind of facts that children liked. He'd just bet her niece and nephew adored her. He could already see the bond she'd formed with his daughter, and how Sienna looked up to her.

It would be all too easy to fall in love

with a woman like Sophie. A woman who'd walked unexpectedly into his life, who was supposed to be his business associate, but who had somehow managed to make him start to feel all the things he'd blocked off since Fran's death. He'd smiled more in the two short weeks he'd known her than he had in the previous two years. And that made him feel antsy. What would happen next? Where did they go from here? It was full of unknowns.

The next stop was the octopus.

'Did you know they have three hearts as well as eight arms?' he asked.

'And they're related to a creature you can see in the garden, especially when it's been a rainy day,' Sophie added. 'Can you guess, Sienna?'

The little girl shook her head. 'Worms?'

'Nearly,' Sophie said, ruffling her hair. 'How about a clue? The creature normally has a spiral shell.'

'Oh—a snail!' Sienna said, smiling.

And funny how her smile made his heart squeeze. Not just because it was so like Fran's, but because she looked happy. And seeing his daughter happy was the best feeling in the world.

They paused in the rock pool area, so Sienna could stroke a starfish and touch an anemone.

'The nennomy looks like a flower,' she said.

The mispronunciation charmed him. 'It's an anemone,' he said. 'Say it after me.' He broke it down into syllables, and Sienna copied him. And then she went back to her original pronunciation. 'The nennomy!'

He smiled, not wanting to spoil her fun by lecturing her. 'It's pretty.'

The area was really crowded, and somehow he ended up sliding his arm round Sophie's shoulders. She turned to glance at him, her dark eyes wide and with a slight flush on her cheeks. Right at that moment, he really, really wanted to kiss her. The thought shocked him deeply; he hadn't felt like that about anyone since Fran.

No way was he going to kiss her in the middle of the crowd, especially with Sienna in front of them. But he had to admit that it was getting more difficult to keep a professional distance between them; and his arm was still round her shoulders when they left the rock pool area. He had to force himself to put a more appropriate distance between them. But then his hand bumped against hers, their fingers tangled together, and for the life of him he couldn't pull away, even though he knew it would be the sensible thing to do.

He gave her a sidelong glance. From the expression on her face, she was feeling the same way: torn between attraction and trying to be professional. Not wanting to take the risk, and yet wanting it at the same time.

Sienna was walking in front of them and clearly hadn't noticed a thing, luckily.

Could they do this?

Should they do this?

He didn't know the answer, but he couldn't stop holding Sophie's hand. And she didn't pull away.

Once they'd seen the displays that Sophie had said were her favourites, the seahorses and the jellyfish, they went to the gift shop.

'What was your favourite animal here, Sienna?' Jamie asked.

His daughter's face was all lit up as she said, 'The penguins!'

'Shall we see if we can find a new bedtime story about penguins?' he asked.

'Yes, please!' Sienna looked thrilled. Jamie glanced at Sophie and the warmth and approval in her eyes made him feel hot all over.

While he and Sienna browsed the bookshelves—and picked up a soft, cuddly penguin at the same time—Sophie found a small penguin wearing a red hat with a white bobble and a loop to hang it from a Christmas tree.

'It's a bit early yet—I never put my Christmas tree up until the first of December,' she said, 'but I'm going to buy you this now so you can put it on your tree when you decorate it, Sienna.'

The little girl was delighted. 'Thank you! Though I'm too little to decorate the tree.'

Jamie saw the surprise that Sophie quickly masked. Clearly her family had different rules from his. When he had been growing up, his mother had always decorated the tree on her own, and Jamie and his sisters had never been involved. His mother liked the tree to look professional, with everything matching and all the baubles spaced the perfect distance apart. He'd ended up doing the same, and even Fran hadn't been able to persuade him out of the habit.

Sophie clearly realised she might have made a gaffe and distracted the little girl. 'Can you help me find a nice present for my niece Hattie and my nephew Sam? Hattie's the same age as you, and her little brother Sam's two. What do you think they might like?'

Sophie helped her to find a soft shark for Sam and a colouring book and pencils for Hattie.

'Perfect choices,' Sophie said. Though Jamie noticed that she still bought the Christmas tree ornament. Given that Cindy wouldn't be back by the first of December, he had a feeling that Sophie intended to make some changes to his routine there, too.

They had dinner together at a restaurant on the south bank, a family-friendly place with a nice children's menu. Sienna chose a quesadilla and a smoothie followed by churros, he and Sophie both opted for a chicken enchilada, and they ordered a bowl of sweet potato fries to share.

When they reached for the fries at the same time and their fingers touched, Jamie felt a frisson of desire all the way down his spine; and he noticed again that Sophie had a slight flush on her cheeks.

It was getting harder and harder to ignore.

Maybe they needed to talk about it. Set out some ground rules. Get things back under control.

'Come back with us and have a glass of wine with me?' he asked when they went to the tube station.

She looked slightly wary.

'You're not driving. Just one glass of wine. No strings,' he said. 'And I'll call you a cab home.'

She paused for so long that he thought she was going to refuse. But then she nodded. 'OK.'

Sienna chattered happily about penguins all the way home.

'I'll put Sienna to bed if you don't mind opening the wine,' Jamie suggested. 'There's a bottle in the fridge.'

Once he'd read the new penguin story to her—twice—he could see Sienna's eyes drooping. 'Time for sleep, now,' he said.

'Love you, Daddy.'

His heart contracted sharply. For the last two years, he'd been wrapped in his grief and had kept his daughter at a distance. And now he realised how much he'd allowed himself to miss out on. He felt a surge of guilt because he'd let his daughter miss out on it, too. 'Love you, too, Sienna.' He kissed her goodnight. 'Sleep tight.'

When he went downstairs, Sophie was sitting on one end of the sofa, with two glasses and the opened bottle of wine on the coffee table.

'Thanks for today,' he said.

'I enjoyed it, too. I always love going there with my niece and nephew.'

He poured them both a glass of wine and sat next to her. 'So are we going to talk about the elephant in the room?'

'That we ended up holding hands in the aquarium?' She blew out a breath. 'I apologise. It was a mistake.'

Which was the right answer. Now they could go back to being professional and pretending it hadn't happened.

Except his mouth had other ideas. 'Was it?'

'If things were different, then maybe not.' She looked away. 'But you have Sienna to think about and you don't need any complications.'

All true. All perfectly valid excuses. Part of him wanted to take them—but a bigger part of him didn't. And if they took this slowly, carefully he could keep his feelings under control.

'Sienna didn't notice anything today. And Sienna doesn't need to know anything right now,' he said. 'This could be just you and me. When she's asleep, or maybe…' He gave her a wry smile. 'I can't believe I'm about to ask you out on a lunch date. I don't even *have* lunch breaks.'

'Exactly. It's too complicated.'

'We could try the simple version,' he suggested.

She shook her head.

But she'd more or less admitted that she felt the same attraction that he did. That in other circumstances she'd consider seeing him. So what was holding her back? 'Why not?'

She sighed. 'It's not you, it's me. I have hopeless judgement in men.'

'So you picked the wrong man. It happens.'

'I spent three years of my life with Dan,' Sophie said. 'How rubbish does that make me?'

'It makes you nice,' he said, 'because you see the best in everyone.' She'd seen something in a man who kept himself safe inside a layer of ice and excuses. And she'd not only seen the best in him, she'd dragged it out, too. He'd resented her for it at times, but he was beginning to see the benefits.

And for Sienna's sake he'd always be grateful to Sophie for that.

'More like a naive idiot, where my love life is concerned,' she said.

He reached over and took her hand, squeezing it briefly and letting it go again to let her know he was on her side. 'You're very far from being an idiot. Is Dan the one who took advantage of you?'

'The first one.' She took a sip of wine. 'I met him in my last year at university—at a party—and I really thought he was the one. We moved in together after we graduated, and I thought we were happy. We were both working slightly mad hours, because I was trying to build my career in event management, and he was training to become an accountant so he was working and studying at the same time. He'd done an economics degree but that didn't exempt him from many exams, so he had to keep going away on some residential course or other.' She grimaced.

'It never even occurred to me that he'd cheat on me while he was away, but it turned out he had a different girl on every course he went on. I didn't often join him at work social events, because they tended to clash with events I was managing—but when I did go to a party with his work friends, I always had this faint suspicion that people were avoiding me. I thought it was just because I wasn't in the same business world and they were being a tiny bit snooty about it, but it turned out to be because they all knew what he was doing and were too embarrassed to talk to me.'

'Which is his fault, not yours.'

'But why didn't I put all the pieces together?' she asked. 'We'd been together for three years when he said he wanted to talk to me. He'd organised dinner out somewhere really flashy. I was so sure he was going to ask me to marry him, because it was actually our third anniversary that night.'

Jamie didn't like where this was going. He had a feeling this was where her heart had been broken. And what kind of lowlife would've done that to a woman like Sophie? It'd be like kicking a puppy or snatching sweeties from a small child.

'Instead, he told me he'd had a fling with someone. A junior in his office. She was pregnant. He said he wasn't in love with her and he didn't want to be with her, but obviously he had to pay child support for the baby.'

It sounded to Jamie as if Dan was the sort who'd try to weasel out of paying child support, too.

'And then he said he'd decided to fight her for custody and he asked me if I'd help him look after the baby.'

He blinked, not quite sure what he was hearing. 'What?'

She looked away. 'I know. How could I have spent three years of my life with someone who was that mean-spirited? The worst thing was, he was shocked when I said no. He thought I was being unreasonable.'

'Hang on.' Jamie could barely process this. 'This is the man who had a fling, wanted to fight the woman for custody so he wouldn't have to pay her anything, and expected you to look after the baby he'd had with someone else—and he said *you* were being unreasonable?'

She grimaced. 'We had a massive fight. He said I was being selfish. And that's when it came out about all the rest of the women he'd cheated on me with. I just walked out of the restaurant and called Eva. She met me at my flat with her car, and we moved all my stuff to her place. She reminded me to call the bank and put a freeze on our joint account so he couldn't just empty all the money into another account, and then I got my name taken off the rent. It was pretty toxic for a while, but I did the right thing. If I'd forgiven him and stayed, I know he would've cheated on me again within the next month.'

'What happened to the baby?' Jamie asked.

'Apparently he's living happily with his mum and her parents. Dan didn't get very far with his custody case—and I don't think he even sees the baby.'

'He sounds like the worst kind of guy,' Jamie said, 'but not all men are like that.'

'I know,' she said softly. 'I have two brothers and a stepdad who are fabulous, and Eva's fiancé Aidan is lovely.'

'But?'

She sighed. 'Dan wasn't my worst mistake—just the first one.'

He waited, knowing that if he gave her enough space she'd eventually talk.

She took another sip of wine. 'I met Joe in a coffee shop. He sent a choc-chip muffin over to me via the waitress, and then we got chatting and he asked me out. I thought he was a nice guy. It took me six months to work out that we never saw each other at weekends, I'd never been to his place, he never stayed at my place overnight and we only went out to small places around where I lived. I thought it was because he was busy at work, and so was I.' She grimaced. 'How stupid was I not to realise that he was avoiding places where he might see people he knew? And he never invited me back to his place because he wasn't the single man I thought he was. He was married.' She closed her eyes briefly and shook her head. 'Worse still, it turned out that his wife was pregnant. She had terrible morning sickness— and, instead of supporting her, like any decent guy would, he was having an affair. With me. This time, I was the other woman. And I really hated that. I've been there. I know how horrible it feels to be the one cheated on. But

I was the other woman, Jamie. I let him cheat on her with me.'

'It wasn't your fault.'

'Of course it was. I agreed to go out with him.'

'It's perfectly reasonable to assume that if someone asks you out, they're not involved with anyone else,' Jamie said gently. 'You really weren't the bad guy here.'

'That's not how it feels.'

'If you'd had any idea that he wasn't single, you wouldn't even have accepted the choc-chip muffin,' he said. 'You have integrity.'

'Thank you.' She blew out a breath. 'But after Dan and Joe, I just can't trust my judgement where my love life is concerned.'

'So, what? You're giving up and spending the rest of your life alone?'

She looked at him. 'You make it sound as if I'm a coward.'

'You're afraid to trust your judgement again.'

'I'm not a coward, Jamie. I just don't want to make any more mistakes. I made two pretty bad ones.'

'Everyone makes mistakes,' he said. 'You just try to learn from them. And yours were different mistakes.'

'At root, they were the same. Trusting people I shouldn't have trusted.'

'People who took advantage of your kindness. Which I guess I'm doing, too.'

She shook her head, grimacing. 'That's different. It's for Sienna. And you're not telling me lies.'

No, but he also wasn't telling her the whole truth about Fran's death. Because he didn't want her to dislike him as much as he disliked himself.

But there was one thing he could do. Something she'd done for him, too.

He took the glass from her and placed it on the coffee table. 'Last week, I was maudlin and hating myself and I really needed a hug. You did that for me and it made me feel a whole lot better. This week, I think it's my turn to give you a hug.'

And he wrapped his arms round her, holding her close.

Mistake.

Big mistake.

Because he could smell the vanilla scent of her shower gel and feel the warmth of her skin. And it made him want to push past another boundary and kiss her. To feel how soft her mouth would be against his, how sweet.

No matter how much he told himself that it would be kissing her better, he knew he was being selfish. Putting his own needs before hers. Because Sophie was vulnerable. She'd done nothing wrong—and yet she blamed herself for being duped by a serial cheater and then a selfish charmer who'd broken his marriage vows.

Could he really say that he was a better man than Joe or Dan? He wasn't a cheat or a liar—but he had been responsible for Fran's death. And he'd let his guilt and the pain get in the way of doing what he should've concentrated on, looking after his little girl.

So in his own way he was probably worse.

Sophie could do so much better than him.

Instead of giving in to the urge to kiss her, he let her go. Stroked her face. 'Don't ever change, Sophie. You're kind and you're lovely.'

'A naive, stupid sucker,' she corrected.

'Better to be naive and believe the best of people than be cynical and bitter and think everyone's just out for themselves,' he countered.

'Maybe.' She shook herself. 'I'd better go.'

She'd barely touched her wine, he noticed.

'I'll call you a cab.'

'It's fine. I can get the Tube.'

'I promised I'd call you a cab.'

'If I stayed and had a glass of wine with you. Which I didn't. I'm sorry I wasted your wine.'

He squeezed her hand briefly. 'Don't apologise. It's my fault for pushing you to talk when you didn't want to.'

'I kind of did that to you,' she admitted.

'Yeah. But you were right,' he said. 'Talking helped.'

She didn't look as if it had helped her much, though. She looked as if she regretted what she'd told him. And he really didn't know how to fix it.

'I'll see you on Monday,' she said. 'Call me if you need anything.'

'You, too,' he said. 'And I'm sorry if I made you feel bad. That wasn't my intention.'

'I know. It's just hard to forgive myself for being such a pushover.'

There were things it was harder to forgive yourself for, but he didn't want to go into that. 'Don't change who you are,' he said. 'Have a good Sunday.'

'You, too.'

And he let her go. Before he did something really stupid. Like kissing her.

CHAPTER FIVE

JAMIE ENDED THE call and sighed. He felt a
bit guilty that he needed to ask Sophie for
her help yet again; then again, this was part
of their deal. Had Cindy not broken her leg,
it wouldn't have been an issue because she
would've been looking after Sienna anyway.

However, had Cindy not broken her leg, he
wouldn't have got to know Sophie this well
in the first place. He might not even have in-
vested in Plans & Planes.

But he really, really liked the woman he
was getting to know.

He called her. 'Good morning. Are you
super-busy right now?'

'Why?'

'Because there's a problem I need to sort
out at work—and it's not something I can delegate,' he explained.

'So you want me to look after Sienna?'

'Please,' he said. 'Just for a couple of hours.

And, because I don't want to take complete advantage of you, I'll cook dinner for you tonight.'

'Cheese on toast again?' she teased.

'No. Name it and I'll cook it.' Even as he said the words, he knew he was giving her the chance to challenge him and suggest something outrageous.

'Chicken parmigiana,' she said. 'I'll email you the link to a recipe. I already know you've got all the ingredients in the fridge and the cupboard. And you can bake some jacket potatoes and steam some vegetables to go with them.'

He knew she was testing him and expecting him to say no; she'd clearly already worked out for herself that it was quite a while since he'd bothered cooking anything properly. 'All right—and thank you. See you at half-past two?'

'Sure.'

At half-past two, Sophie arrived with a DVD and a bag full of ingredients. 'This is what rainy Sunday afternoons are for,' she said to Sienna. 'We're going to make dessert and some cookies, and then we'll watch a movie.'

'Yay!' Sienna looked thrilled.

'Thank you for coming,' Jamie said. 'I feel a bit guilty for asking you.'

'It's fine. It's what we agreed,' she reminded him. 'Go and do your work.'

While Jamie was stuck at his computer, he could smell something gorgeous. Vanilla? Chocolate? If he sneaked into the kitchen, would they let him steal a cookie?

Just as he was considering it, there was a quiet knock on his study door, then a louder knock. 'Come in,' he said.

The door opened and Sienna came in, carrying a plate containing a single choc-chip cookie; Sophie followed her, carrying a mug of coffee.

'You made the cookie?' he asked, though he already knew the answer because there was still a smear of flour across his daughter's nose and she was wearing the pink apron with white spots that Sophie had bought her.

'I made it specially for you,' Sienna said proudly.

'It smells absolutely scrumptious.'

She looked worried, as if not sure whether that was a good thing or a bad; clearly she hadn't come across the word before. 'That means "delicious" and I can't wait to try it,' he said with a smile. 'Thank you, Sienna.'

He took a mouthful. The cookie was still warm and it tasted even better than it smelled: buttery and chocolaty with a hint of vanilla.

'Is it all right?' Sienna asked, still looking worried.

'It's the best cookie I've ever had in my whole life,' he said. 'Thank you, darling. Can I have another one, please?'

She beamed. 'Yes! As long as you promise to eat your dinner.'

He wasn't sure whether that was Cindy's influence or Sophie's, and had to hide a grin. 'I promise.'

She brought him another cookie. 'We're going to watch a movie now, all about a princess.'

'Sounds good,' he said. 'Have fun.'

She smiled again, waved him a shy goodbye, and trotted off with Sophie.

Even though Jamie was concentrating on his file, he could hear the faint sound of music in the background—clearly something from the movie. Then he heard Sophie singing along with the music; she had a really good voice. He heard Sienna's higher voice joining in with part of the chorus, and then he heard Sophie say, 'Let's rewind the movie a bit and sing it again together.'

He couldn't resist tiptoeing out to the hall and peeking into the living room.

Sienna and Sophie weren't just singing, they were dancing in front of the television and clearly having a wonderful time. And they didn't look anything like temporary nanny and her charge: they looked like a family.

This was the sort of thing Fran would've done with Sienna. The sort of thing *he* should've done, in Fran's absence, instead of letting his own childhood get in the way. Gwen Wallis had been a great believer in children being seen and not heard, and he'd followed in his mother's footsteps. But, since Sophie had come into his life, Jamie had discovered that actually he liked the sound of hearing his little girl giggling and singing.

Once Cindy came back, there would definitely be some changes made to their routine—changes he knew Cindy had tried to implement before, but he'd been too wrapped up in his grief and his guilt to let her make them.

Guilt still froze him, but he knew it was time to think about moving on. It was time to make Sienna's world a better place: starting with cooking dinner for them all tonight.

And Sophie? Last night, she'd made it very clear she wasn't looking for a relationship. He could understand why; she'd dated a couple of men who'd treated her badly and had made her think it was her fault, when in reality it had been their problem rather than hers. Maybe he could help her see that it wasn't her fault—and that maybe it was worth dating again. And that maybe it would be worth dating him...

He shook himself. They'd known each other a fortnight, that was all. This was all happening much too soon. Then again, she was the first person who'd really got through to him since Fran. Her warmth and her openness were irresistible, and he hadn't been able to help responding to her, even though his head was telling him that he shouldn't give in to the crazy impulses—that would lead to falling in love and losing control of his emotions.

Sophie Firth was special.

Jamie went back to his office and finished sorting things out, then cooked dinner. Just as Sophie had promised, all the ingredients were in the fridge. Funny, cooking dinner for them made him feel as if he was really part of a family. He was horribly aware he'd always left the cooking to Fran because she'd enjoyed it and he wasn't bothered either way; he'd been happy to deal with the household chores that she hated instead. But this... This was very different.

Was this the second chance he'd wanted deep down but had thought was unobtainable?

Was Sophie the one who could redeem him?

He shook himself. Once she knew the truth about Fran's death, she'd back off. It was pointless even trying. Better to keep things strictly professional.

He went into the living room. 'OK. Dinner's ready in five minutes. Come and wash your hands.'

Despite his resolutions, the warmth in Sophie's smile curled deep inside him, melting another layer of ice from round his heart.

'This is scrumshuss, Daddy,' Sienna said after her first taste, clearly wanting to use her newly learned word.

'It's good,' Sophie added with a smile. 'OK. I believe you now. You can cook.'

But when she retrieved dessert from the freezer, he realised she'd more than outdone him.

'Are those *penguins*?' he asked.

'Banana penguins,' she confirmed with a grin. 'I thought after yesterday these would be perfect. It's really easy to make them—you just dip the banana in melted chocolate, make the feet and beak out of dried apricots, and use marshmallows and chocolate chips for the eyes.'

'We maked the penguins before we maked the cookies,' Sienna said gleefully.

So that must've been what some of the giggling was about. He didn't have the heart to correct his daughter's grammar. 'I'm impressed.'

'Not my idea,' Sophie admitted with a smile. 'I don't think it was even my sister-in-law's, actually. I think she got it from the Internet.'

'They're great,' he said. He would never have thought of them in a million years.

The banana penguins were a total hit, and Sienna chattered about them all the way through bathtime—and even though he still insisted on shallow baths, he could manage bathtimes now without flashbacks.

Jamie read three stories to Sienna, then headed downstairs to join Sophie.

'I feel bad about you doing the washing up,' he said, noticing that she'd put everything away neatly as well.

'Hey. You cooked. In my book, that lets you off dishwashing duty,' she said with a smile.

'Can I get you a glass of wine or a coffee?'

'Thanks, but I need to be going,' she said. 'This is Hattie's favourite film of all time and I promised to take it back tonight.'

'OK. Thanks again for today,' he said.

'My pleasure.'

'Seriously—you saved my bacon and you make Sienna happy. It's good to see her laughing.'

'She'd be like this with Cindy.' Sophie paused and looked him straight in the eye. 'And with her grandparents.'

Not his own parents. He couldn't imagine them dancing or singing. 'Fran's parents live quite a way away.'

'And you have guest rooms,' she pointed out. 'They could stay for the weekend. Or midweek. Whatever works for you all.

'I...' He sighed. He knew she saw right through him and she'd counter any excuse she made. 'You're right. It's an excuse. But every time I look at Fran's mother, I see Fran.'

'And it hurts? I get that,' she said. 'But there has to be a point where the good memories start to take over. When you start to remember Fran with smiles instead of tears. Would she have wanted you and Sienna to be miserable for the rest of your lives?'

'No,' he admitted.

'Then think about it. Sienna needs more than just you and Cindy in her life,' she said gently. 'And, take it from me, it's lovely to see your parents playing with the generation below yours, singing the same songs you remember them singing to you and telling the same terrible jokes.'

'What if you don't remember your parents singing to you and telling you jokes?' The words came out before he could stop them.

She reached up to stroke his face. 'That's when you get to teach them how to do it. How to loosen up and have fun.'

Even Fran hadn't been able to make him loosen up totally, so Jamie knew he didn't have a chance in hell of making his parents loosen up. Even now, despite heading towards the age when they really ought to retire and enjoy their lives, they were still focused on work and the business, and he was really glad he'd struck out on his own rather than agreeing to take over from them—because he was pretty sure neither of them intended to retire. 'Maybe,' he said, trying to be diplomatic.

But her hand was still against his face. His skin tingled where she touched him. How could he resist twisting his head slightly so he could press a kiss into her palm?

Her dark eyes widened—with shock or desire? he wondered.

He wanted to kiss her properly.

But it was too soon. Instead, he took her

hand and folded her fingers over the place where he'd kissed her. 'Goodnight, Sophie. See you tomorrow,' he said.

'Tomorrow,' she said. Was it his imagination, or was her voice slightly husky?

Sophie was glad she was driving, because it meant she had to concentrate on the way to her brother and sister-in-law's instead of letting herself dream about Jamie Wallis and brooding over the way he'd kissed her palm. She managed to sidestep all mentions of Jamie when she was sitting in their living room, drinking tea and enjoying their company. But all too soon she was back in her flat and the pictures in her head wouldn't go away.

What would it be like if Jamie kissed her properly? Kissed her like a lover?

She shivered. This was a bad idea. He was vulnerable; he was still hurting over his wife's death to the point where he had trouble spending time with anyone who reminded him of Fran. And even though she knew that Jamie wouldn't lie to her and cheat on her, the way Dan and Joe had, she still thought anything more than a professional relationship between them would be a disaster.

The problem was, when he'd kissed her

palm, she'd almost stepped forward and kissed his mouth.

Jamie Wallis was gorgeous with a capital G.

And she really would have to keep reminding herself that he was off limits.

Over the next few days Sophie and Sienna started making things to prepare for Christmas. An advent calendar with pockets for little gifts, which Sophie planned to pick up at the same time that her sister-in-law bought gifts for her own advent calendars for Hattie and Sam; home-made decorations for the Christmas tree, painting yogurt pots with metallic paint and sprinkling glitter on them and making a hanging loop from a tinsel pipe cleaner; and a home-made photo frame made from macaroni stuck onto cardboard and covered with spray paint.

Jamie discovered 'stained glass windows' on various windows around the house, made from black sugar paper with shapes cut out and coloured tissue paper stuck over the gaps to create the 'stained glass'. And there was a painting of a Christmas tree made out of handprints, and an angel with wings made out of handprints—all things that he knew Fran would've enjoyed doing with their daughter. Things he wouldn't even know how to start doing.

And every day his daughter came more and more out of her shell, laughing and smiling and responding to Sophie's warmth.

He really wasn't sure whether he was more charmed or terrified by it. But everything in his house felt different. *Better.*

How could Sophie have changed everything so much in three short weeks?

And where did they go from here?

On Saturday afternoon, Sophie and Jamie took Sienna to the Natural History Museum.

'I can remember coming here with my parents when I was tiny,' Sophie said. 'My brothers were dinosaur-mad. They loved it here. Whenever Mum asked us where we wanted to go for an afternoon out, Matt and Will always wanted to come here.'

'What about you?' he asked.

'Oh, me, too. My favourite was the triceratops because of its frilly neck. And we all nagged and nagged to go to Lyme Regis on holiday, in case we found a dinosaur on the beach.'

'Did you really find a dinosaur?' Sienna asked, her eyes wide.

'No, but we did find some fossils.' She

smiled. 'I still have the first ammonite I ever found.'

'What's a nammo…?' Sienna stumbled over the name.

'An ammonite was a sea creature with a spiral shell, a bit like a snail's shell but bigger,' Sophie explained. 'I can show you one here.'

They wandered round the exhibition together, and Sophie came out with a stream of terrible dinosaur jokes. 'Sienna, what do you call a sleeping dinosaur?'

'I don't know,' Sienna said, playing along.

'A Stego-snorus!' Sophie told her with a grin.

And when they got to the scary animatronic Tyrannosaurus Rex and Sienna started to look worried, Sophie squeezed her hand. 'Which dinosaur had to wear glasses?'

'I don't know.'

'Is Daddy going to guess?'

'Nope,' Jamie said.

'You're going to groan,' she warned. 'Wait for it… The Tyrannosaurus Specs!'

But she saved her most terrible one until last. 'Where does a Triceratops sit?' When Sienna shook her head, Sophie grinned. 'On its Tricera-bottom!'

The joke had Sienna giggling like mad, and even Jamie couldn't help smiling.

'You can blame my mum for those,' she said with a grin. 'She's the one who taught me them.'

Jamie couldn't remember his mother—or his father—ever telling a joke, much less the sort that a child would appreciate. He pushed the thought away. He didn't have to be like his parents. He was pretty sure that his sisters weren't like their parents—even though he hadn't seen either of his sisters for months, using the excuse that they lived just too far away. But Sophie had shown him that all he had to do was to be himself.

In one of the exhibition rooms, they found themselves in a queue where they were slightly squished together, just as it had been last week; and it felt natural to Jamie to slide his arm round Sophie's shoulder and hold her close, protecting her from the squash. She didn't pull away, and even when the queue thinned out again her fingers ended up curling round his.

Maybe this was the way forward. Baby steps negotiated quietly, instead of big declarations.

When Sienna had had her fill of the museum, they found a family-friendly restaurant. 'It's my turn to pay, so don't argue,' he informed Sophie outside the restaurant.

'OK. Thank you.'

And it really felt like a family meal out. He noticed the way Sophie was with his daughter, encouraging her and drawing her out, and Sienna responded to Sophie's warmth. He was aware that it was the same for him, too; part of him was flustered by his growing feelings for her, but part of him wanted more. Much more.

Back at the house, she made coffee while he settled Sienna in bed, and was curled up on a corner of the sofa, doing something on her phone, when he came downstairs.

'Hey.' He sat next to her and took her hand.

She looked wary. 'I thought we agreed last week that this would be a bad idea.'

'It is,' he said. 'But I can't stop thinking about you. And I've got a feeling it might be the same for you.' Because otherwise why had they ended up holding hands in the museum, earlier that day?

She blew out a breath. 'I'm rubbish at relationships, and you're vulnerable.'

Both statements were true; but both things could be changed. 'So maybe we should just muddle through this together and see how it works out,' he said. 'Humour me.'

'Humour you, how?' she asked.

'Like this,' he said, and leaned over to brush

his mouth against hers. Just once. Not demanding, not threatening, just letting her know how he felt. Leaving the next move to her.

Sophie couldn't remember the last time someone had kissed her properly.

She certainly couldn't remember the last time someone had made her knees feel weak in two seconds flat.

And that kiss, even though it had been sweet and gentle and had left the next move up to her, had made every nerve-end in her lips tingle.

'We can't do this,' she said, resting her palm against his face.

Big mistake. Now her hand was tingling as much as her mouth. And she wanted to slide her hand into his hair and draw his face down to hers. Kiss him back.

'This is a really bad idea,' he said, his voice deep and husky and sexy as hell.

His mouth was saying one thing, but his eyes were saying something different. Tempting her to kiss him back, to hold him.

She wasn't sure which of them moved first, but then somehow she was sitting on his lap, his arms were wrapped round her, her hands were in his hair and his mouth was jammed against hers.

When Jamie broke the kiss, Sophie couldn't speak. All her words, her protests, her common sense had been driven clean out of her head.

'This is insane,' she said at last.

'Absolutely,' he agreed, and ran the pad of his thumb along her lower lip.

The next thing she knew, her lips had parted and he was kissing her again. As if he was trying to be sensible but he just couldn't resist her.

Which was how it felt when she kissed him back. He was irresistible.

'You… I… This is all too complicated,' she said.

He stroked her hair. 'Or maybe it's simple. Maybe it's just about you and me.'

'What about Sienna? What about Plans & Planes? What about…?' Her words dried up as he caught her lower lip gently between his teeth.

And then she stopped thinking and kissed him again.

'Sienna doesn't need to know about this until we're ready to tell her,' he said when she broke the kiss. 'And we're both sensible enough to keep business and personal separate. Whatever this thing is between us, it has nothing to do with business.'

'Agreed.'

'I don't know where this is going. I don't know what I can offer you. Part of me is scared because I'm used to being in control of my thoughts and my feelings,' he admitted. 'But I like the way you make me feel. And I don't want that to stop.'

Sophie had thought everything was simple with Joe and with Dan—and it had turned out to be nastily complicated. So maybe Jamie was right about this thing between them and this was the complete opposite: it looked complicated at first glance, but at heart it was simple.

'So we take this day by day,' she said. 'No promises.'

'Sounds good to me.' He kissed her again. 'And nobody else needs to know, until we've worked out what we're doing.'

'Agreed.'

'I haven't felt like this in a very long time,' he said softly.

'Me neither.'

'So we'll take it slowly,' he said, and gently set her back off his lap and on the sofa next to him.

Kissing. Holding hands. Sort-of dating.

'I feel like a teenager,' she confessed.

'Me, too.' He gave her a wry smile. 'Until

Cindy's back at work, I can't date you the way I'd like to. I can't take you dancing, or out to dinner, or any of the more traditional things.'

'That's OK. I've been enjoying what we do with Sienna.' She gave him a sidelong glance. 'And we can do dancing here.'

'Is that an offer of a slow dance, or what you were doing with her in front of that movie?'

She groaned. 'Don't tell me you saw that?'

'Yup,' he said with a smile. 'You both looked happy. As if you were having fun.'

'We were. Next time, you ought to join us,' she said.

'Maybe I will. The next rainy Sunday afternoon.' He stole another kiss. 'And when it's a rainy Sunday night and Sienna's asleep, then it's just you and me dancing. To something slow and sweet.'

'I'll hold you to that,' she said. She kissed him again, then stood up. 'And I need to go.' While she still could.

On Sunday morning, Jamie had a project meeting, so Sophie picked Sienna up and took her to the park to meet up with her sister-in-law, niece and nephew.

'This is my niece Hattie, who's the same

age as you, and her little brother Sam,' Sophie introduced them. 'And this is their mum, Mandy.'

'Hello,' Sienna said shyly.

'Let's go on the swings,' Hattie said, taking her hand.

Sienna glanced at Sophie for direction, and Sophie smiled and inclined her head.

Hattie immediately started chatting to her, and Sophie followed with Mandy and Sam.

'She clearly adores you,' Mandy said, 'and from the look on her face it's obvious you adore her.'

'She's a lovely little girl,' Sophie said.

'Even so. Be careful,' Mandy warned.

'I know. He's off limits. My business partner.' Sophie had explained the situation to Mandy just after she'd agreed to be Sienna's temporary nanny. 'And he's vulnerable. He was widowed really young, remember.'

'From what you've told me over the last couple of weeks,' Mandy said thoughtfully, 'it sounds to me as if you're falling in love with both him and Sienna.'

Sophie had a nasty feeling that her sister-in-law was right, but shook her head. 'I've learned my lesson after Dan and Joe. I'm not going to lose my heart to anyone ever again.'

'Just be careful, that's all,' Mandy said. 'I don't want to see you hurt again.'

'I promise,' Sophie said, crossing her fingers surreptitiously behind her back. She certainly wasn't going to tell Mandy about the hand-holding yesterday and the kissing last night.

The little girls insisted on going on every single piece of equipment in the park, from the swings to the see-saw to the slides and the bouncy chickens on enormous springs. Sophie took pictures on her phone of the little girls on the slide together, and another one of herself and Sienna at the top of the big slide, holding hands and ready to zoom down to the bottom.

And when they were finally done and Sam was starting to get just a little bit grizzly, they went to the café at the edge of the park for brunch.

'Pancakes and milkshake for me, please,' Hattie said before they'd even looked at the menu.

'And me, please,' Sienna added.

'Pancakes!' Sam beamed at them.

'Pancakes all round, I think,' Mandy said with a smile. 'Sophie, a cappuccino for you?'

'Yes, please.' Sophie stood up and patted her shoulder. 'I'll go and sort it all out if you don't mind staying here with the children.'

The café had colour-in menus, and the girls had just finished colouring them in neatly, while Sam scribbled exuberantly over his, when their drinks and a stack of pancakes arrived.

'I think the girls have just found their new best friend,' Mandy said quietly to Sophie. 'If Jamie's OK with it, maybe Sienna would like to come and play over at our place next weekend.'

'I'll check with him and let you know, but I can't see a problem,' Sophie said. 'It's nice that they get on so well.'

After a second round of milkshakes and coffee, they headed for home.

Sienna was quiet, and Sophie assumed she'd tired herself out at the park and had fallen asleep in the car. But when she glanced at the little girl, she realised that Sienna was crying silently.

'Sweetie, what's wrong?' she asked.

'I wish I had a mummy like Hattie does,' Sienna said, sniffing.

'Oh, darling. I know it's been hard for you.' And then Sophie realised she hadn't even seen a photograph of Fran in the house. She was going to have to tackle Jamie about this, even if it meant wrecking the fragile beginnings of what was happening between them. She could tell Sienna until she was blue in the face that her mother had loved her dearly, but without physical proof—photographs and videos—the little girl's doubts would remain. 'But your dad loves you very, very much.' And he was going to get a lot better at showing it, if Sophie had anything to do with it.

When they got back to the house, Sienna's tears had dried, but the evidence was still there in the puffiness of her eyes.

'What happened?' Jamie mouthed over the top of his daughter's head.

'Tell you later,' she mouthed back.

'So where did you go this morning?' Jamie asked.

'We went to the park and then we had pancakes,' Sienna said. 'I made a new friend. Her name's Hattie. She's the same age as me and her favourite colour's pink, too.'

He raised an eyebrow at Sophie. 'You took her to meet your family?'

'I usually spend some of the weekend with my family,' she corrected, 'and meeting them at the park meant I got to see them as well as spend time with Sienna. The girls had a great time.' She took her phone out of her bag and showed him the photographs. 'I'm going to print some of these out when I get home, Sienna, so you can stick them on your fridge with magnets.'

'Come and tell me about the park and your pancakes,' Jamie said. 'And then I'll read you a story.'

Sienna obligingly told him about every single piece of equipment she'd been on, but he was only halfway through the story when she fell asleep on him.

Gently, he stood up, still cradling her, then set her back on the sofa and tucked a blanket round her. Then he pointed to the kitchen.

Sophie nodded and followed him.

'So what happened?' he asked, keeping his voice quiet.

Sophie blew out a breath. 'I'm so sorry, Jamie. I feel horrible that she got so upset. She saw Mandy and Hattie being close, like any other mum and daughter, and it made her miss Fran.' She bit her lip. 'She said on the way home that she wished she had a mummy.'

Jamie went white.

'Look, I don't want to make things worse, but there isn't a single picture of Fran in your house,' she said.

'Because it hurts to look at them,' he said.

'I get that,' she said softly, 'but not having anything at all is hurting Sienna. Right now, I think she needs to know that her mum loved her. Or am I missing something here? Was Fran maybe not the maternal type?'

He shook his head. 'Fran loved her. Loved her more than anything.'

'Then Sienna needs to know that, Jamie. Even if it hurts you to see the pictures, she needs to see them so she can see that love for herself. She needs to see pictures of her and her mum together—video, too, if you've got it.'

'I...' He sounded as if the words had just choked him.

'Would it help you if I went through the photos with you and picked some out?' And she really hoped he realised that she was trying to be supportive rather than pushy.

He swallowed hard. 'Maybe.'

'Did Fran have a baby book?'

He nodded. 'I put it away in a box, along with the wedding photos.'

'Sienna needs to see it,' Sophie said gently. 'She's really careful with things, so she won't damage it. But she needs to know it exists and her mum loved her.'

'Come into the office,' he said.

He switched on his computer and they went through the files of photographs together.

'She's so like Sienna,' Sophie said. Those same blonde curls and sweet smile.

He nodded. 'That's why I...'

She mentally filled in the rest. Why he'd found it so hard to be with his daughter, because she was a constant reminder of what he'd lost. And Sophie had pushed him and pushed him and pushed him.

'Fran's very beautiful,' Sophie said.

'And she was nice. Funny. Sweet. She made me a better man,' he said. 'And when we had Sienna, I thought life couldn't get any better. I was so happy. Our little family... It wasn't like I remember things being when I was a small child. It was different.'

A close, loving family like her own, Sophie thought, rather than the cold, old-fashioned family Cindy had confided to her about.

He dragged in a breath. 'Two weeks before we went to the Caribbean, Fran told me she was pregnant. Six weeks. Sienna was going to have a little brother or sister.'

So he hadn't just lost his wife. He'd lost a child as well. No wonder he was still hurting for the might-have-beens. She wrapped her arms round him. 'That's hard. I'm so sorry.'

'Every time I look at Sienna, I see what might have been. And I hate myself for it.'

'But you can't live in the past, or in what might have been,' she said softly. 'Live in the here and now. Look at what you have. Sienna's the sweetest, sweetest little girl. And she loves you dearly.'

'How can she, when I hardly spend time with her?'

'She loves you,' Sophie repeated. 'And you love her.'

'Of course I do. She's part of me. And I'm letting her down.'

'Things are changing,' she said. 'You're spending more time with her now and it's going to get easier every day. And then you'll get to the point where you see what you have now, instead of what you lost. You're making good memories together. The fireworks and the dinosaurs and the painting and the stories.'

'Uh-huh.'

He didn't look convinced, and her heart bled for him. She held him more tightly, just for a second. 'It's going to be OK, Jamie. Really, it is. Now let's find some photographs of Sienna with Fran and print them out. Maybe you can make a collage together and put them in a frame in her room.'

His eyes were wet, as if he'd been blinking back tears. 'I should've done that before.'

'I don't think you were in the right place to do it before,' she said gently. 'But you are now. And it's going to be OK. I promise.'

CHAPTER SIX

On Monday morning, Sienna was bright and chirpy. 'Come and see what Daddy and me makes,' she said, tugging at Sophie's hand.

Up in Sienna's bedroom, there was a new frame on the wall; either Jamie had recycled it from somewhere or he'd managed to find a craft place still open when Sienna had woken yesterday after her nap.

And the frame was filled with a collage of photos of Sienna with Fran.

'My mummy's in heaven but Daddy says she still loves me, even though I can't see her,' Sienna said, 'and he says every time I look up and see the stars twinkling it's to show me she's smiling down at me.'

Sophie had to blink back a rush of tears. 'Yes, he's right.'

'So I do have a mummy like Hattie.'

'You do, darling.' Sophie couldn't help hugging her.

Later that night, when Jamie came down-stairs after reading Sienna's bedtime story, she hugged him.

'What was that for?' he asked.

'What you did for Sienna. Even though I know it must've been like sprinkling salt in your wounds.'

'It was,' he admitted. 'But for her sake I should've done it a long while ago.'

'You've done it now. And that's a really good thing.'

He stole a kiss. 'Thanks to you.'

She stroked his face. 'Hey. I didn't do much.'

'Yes, you did. You gave me the strength to face something I found really tough,' he said, 'and I appreciate it. I know I ought to let you go, but come and sit with me for a while?'

'OK.'

He led her over to the sofa in the living room, then drew her onto his lap. 'So how's it going with Plans & Planes?'

'Good. Georgia and Lily have both settled in really well, and Georgia's been excellent at dealing with the events side.' She smiled at him. 'This isn't really the appropriate place to say this, but I'd really like to poach both of them permanently.'

'I have a half-stake in the business,' he

said, 'so if moving staff around between the two businesses means an increase in productivity, that's fine.'

'I haven't asked them yet,' she warned.

'I'll talk to Karen and prime her that you're going to ask—and if they want to move across permanently, it's fine.'

'Thanks.'

'You're really going to miss Eva, aren't you?' he asked.

'She's been my best friend for eleven years—a huge part of my life,' Sophie said. 'But we can do video calls, and still send each other texts and emails. And I have work to keep me busy.'

'Two jobs, at the moment,' he said, looking faintly guilty.

'Two half-jobs,' she corrected. 'And I know we were talking about Plans & Planes, but I'm going to switch hats. It's December next week.'

Jamie groaned. 'I have a nasty feeling I know what's coming next. You want to do the tree.'

'Yup.'

He sighed. 'I'd kind of noticed the homemade ornaments appearing on all the windowsills.'

'It was a bit of a hint. Kids love helping to

decorate the tree.' Then a nasty thought hit her. 'Or do you have a problem with Christmas?'

'No more than any other day of the year,' he said.

But he seemed reluctant and she couldn't work out why. 'Didn't you used to decorate the tree with your parents?'

'No,' he said shortly.

More of that ridiculously Victorian 'children should be seen and not heard' business? she wondered. 'OK. Maybe it's time to start making some new traditions with Sienna,' she said carefully.

'You're not going to give in until I agree, are you?' he asked wryly.

'That would be a no.'

He rolled his eyes, though she noticed that he was smiling—so he couldn't be too put out by her suggestion. 'OK. I'll finish early on Friday and pick her up from nursery and choose a tree.'

'A real tree, not an artificial one.'

'A real tree.' He paused. 'Would you come with us?'

She grinned. 'I'd love to.'

'You're one of these people who really loves Christmas, aren't you?'

'Yes. It's the best day of the year.' She frowned. 'Don't you?'

'It's just another day. And the holidays are way too commercial.'

'Christmas is what you make it,' she said firmly. 'In my family, we give each other token presents and spoil the children. Sam's getting a train set this year—Will and Mandy have bought a massive wooden track, and the rest of us have bought trains or accessories. We're doing the same with Hattie's doll's house. And I'm pretty sure all of us are going to be on the floor, playing with them. And then there will be the board games, and someone will decide to change the rules, and there will be forfeits involved—probably involving cake and chocolate.'

He said nothing, not being drawn on what Christmas was usually like for him and Sienna. She guessed that since Fran's death it had been a very, very quiet affair.

'You could,' she said quietly, 'come and join us if you want to. There's plenty of room and my mum always cooks way too much food.'

'You're inviting us for Christmas?' He looked shocked. 'But won't your parents mind?'

She shrugged. 'The way Mum sees it, the more, the merrier.'

'I...' He blinked, as if he couldn't quite take it in.

'You don't have to say yes right now. Think about it.'

'How would you introduce us?'

She smiled. 'My family already knows about you both.'

His eyes widened. 'Do they know...?'

'About you and me? No. They just know you bought Eva's share of the business and I'm helping you out on the nanny front. And obviously Mandy, Hattie and Sam have met Sienna.'

'Uh-huh.' He seemed to relax.

'You and me—that's just between us. Because it's still very early days,' she said. 'As far as everyone else is concerned, you and I are business associates and are sort of getting to know each other as friends.'

'Friends.' He stole a kiss.

'And I'm going with you to choose the tree on Friday simply as your friend.'

Friends. He thought about it. They *were* becoming friends. He liked Sophie a lot, as well as being attracted to her.

But friendship plus attraction added up to a very different sum. One that scared him.

Could he trust her with his battered heart? Could he relinquish control and let himself love her?

She kissed him back. 'I need to go. But I'll see you tomorrow. Have a think about Christmas. No pressure—I won't say a word to Sienna.'

On Friday afternoon, Jamie and Sophie took Sienna to the garden centre to choose a Christmas tree together. Sienna and Sophie made a beeline for the tree decorations, and Jamie didn't get a chance to say that he already had decorations, because Sienna was oohing and ahhing over the most glittery things. Even though the things that she picked out made him wince inwardly at their garishness, there was no way he could say no. Particularly as Sophie took the basket and insisted on paying.

Sophie suggested they put the tree in the living room, the furthest distance from the radiators and the fire. 'Because then it won't dry out,' she said.

And then they proceeded to decorate the tree together.

It was so different from the tree he usually had, with its matching colour scheme and the baubles a regulation distance apart and sober white lights. Sophie had bought gaudy coloured lights that flashed in different patterns, and Sienna was thrilled by them. Jamie gritted his teeth and looped the lights around the branches, starting from the top.

The elegant glass baubles he normally used were replaced by a mixture of Sienna's painted yoghurt pots and the glittery decorations she'd found at the garden centre, plus the penguin with the Christmas hat they'd bought at the aquarium.

It looked terrible. A complete mess. Every sinew in his body screamed to put some sort of order to it.

But his daughter was smiling. So he didn't say a word.

'We need to put the star at the top, Daddy.' Sienna produced a cardboard star that she'd painted gold and then sprinkled golden glitter on it.

There was a gold ribbon secured to the back of the star so he could tie it to the tree.

'That's perfect, Daddy. It's the Bethlehem star.' Sienna beamed and sang 'Twinkle, Twinkle Little Star'.

Jamie had the biggest lump in his throat and he couldn't say a word.

'Sienna, can you stand in front of the tree

and sing that for me again, please, sweetie?'
Sophie asked.

Sienna obliged, scrunching her hands up
and opening them wide to the word 'twinkle'.

'That's the song Bethany asked me to sing
in the Christmas concert,' she said.

'Because you sing it so beautifully,' Sophie added.

'Sophie's making me angel wings for the
concert,' Sienna said, doing a little happy
wiggle. 'And a halo.'

Couldn't she just buy a proper costume
in a shop? Jamie wondered. But he glanced
at Sophie before he said it, and clearly she'd
guessed what he was thinking because she
gave the tiniest shake of her head to warn
him to shut up.

'That's lovely, darling,' he said instead.

'And now I want a picture of you both in
front of the tree,' Sophie said, 'for Cindy.'

'I want you in the picture, too, Sophie,' Sienna said.

'Let's have one with you and Daddy, and
then one with all three of us,' Sophie suggested.

'Yay!' Sienna said with a smile.

Sophie took a few shots on her phone, then
said to Sienna, 'Do you want to help me send
this picture of you and Daddy to Cindy?'

'And to the grannies,' Sienna added.

Grannies? What was going on? Jamie gave Sophie a suspicious look.

'Later,' she mouthed.

He waited until after Sienna's bedtime story to tackle Sophie. 'Right. Explain about the grannies.'

She sighed. 'It's nothing so terrible. I just send her grandmothers photos of Sienna and bits of her artwork.'

'Both of them?'

'Both of them,' she confirmed.

He narrowed his eyes at her. 'That's not in your remit.'

'You didn't say I couldn't,' she pointed out.

'How did you get their details?'

She mimed a zip across her mouth. 'I'm taking the Fifth on that one.'

He scoffed. 'You can't, because you're not American and we don't have a constitution.'

'In that case, I'm not telling you, because then there can't be any comebacks,' she said. She narrowed her eyes at him. 'And there *mustn't* be any comebacks, Jamie.'

He was pretty sure that Cindy must have given her the information. 'I can't believe—'

'Stop being so prissy,' Sophie cut in. 'Sienna's their granddaughter. All grandparents love getting their grandkids' artwork and sticking it on the fridge. And, for your information, they loved the pictures I sent them of you two with the dinosaurs last week.'

'Hang on. This is my mother you're talking about, too?' he checked, not quite believing it.

'Yup. Granny Gwen and Granny Rose.'

'And my mother hasn't given you a list of detailed instructions about Sienna?'

'No,' Sophie said. 'Well, she tried. Then I explained to her I'm not actually your employee.' The corner of her mouth twitched. 'And that actually I'm bossier than she is.'

He rolled his eyes. 'Hardly.'

'Oh, but I am. Look at that tree. It's there—even though you hate it,' she said, 'and you're quivering and desperate to make everything all neat and regulated and subtle.'

'Well—yes,' he admitted.

'Which isn't what Christmas is all about, Jamie. Christmas is about having fun, about singing carols and pop songs, about having chocolate for breakfast and the dog having his share of Christmas dinner and then spending the afternoon farting in the living room because he's scoffed too much turkey. It's about games for the whole family, and tinsel, and really terrible cracker jokes, and paper hats.'

Jamie just looked at her, unable to think of a way to counteract anything she said.

'Oh, though I do have one regulation for next weekend,' she said with a smile. 'You're taking Sienna to see Father Christmas.'

'Right.' This was the first he'd heard of it.

She gave him the cheekiest grin. 'I've booked it and paid for it—I've got a time slot and everything. So that will soothe your soul about sticking to regulations.'

'Now you're mocking me.'

She walked over to him and kissed him lightly. 'I am. Because you're being pompous and you deserve to be mocked for that.'

And the touch of her mouth did more to silence him than anything she'd said.

Her phone beeped to signal an incoming text. She glanced at the screen, grinned, and handed the phone to him. 'Righty. Read this.'

The sender turned out to be his mother.

Oh, how sweet!

Gwen followed it up with a second message.

Twinkle, Twinkle. That was Jamie's favourite song at that age.

Jamie stared at the words, open-mouthed. 'Are you sure we're not in a parallel universe?

How would she even know that? I don't remember my parents ever coming to school concerts when I was small. They were always working.' Just like he was, he thought with a twinge of guilt.

'But I bet they had a video camera—right from when they were really new on the market and hideously expensive,' Sienna said. 'And my guess is your dad taught your nanny how to use it and got her to film you and your sisters at all the things he and your mum didn't manage to get to.'

Now he thought about it, Jamie could remember their nanny using an expensive camera. But even so. 'My mother…' He blew out a breath. 'That text can't possibly be from her.' It didn't sound like her. Fond. Warm. Loving. Soft. That wasn't his mother at all.

'It is. Call her and talk to her, if you like. And, while you're at it, ask her to come to the nursery school Christmas concert. I bet you she'll say yes.'

He shook his head. 'She'll be too busy at work.'

'Ask her,' Sophie said again.

Another message came in. He looked at the screen. 'You've got a text from Rose.' Fran's mother.

'Read it to me,' she said.

There was a lump in his throat making him croak as he read the words. 'It says, "She looks just like my Frannie. Thank you, Sophie." And there are three kisses.'

'I know you think you have to do this all on your own, with the support of a nanny—but you don't,' she said softly. 'It's coming up to Christmas. Give everyone a chance, Jamie.'

He scowled at her. 'I suppose you're going to suggest now I have everyone here for Christmas.'

'That's an even more brilliant idea than coming to spend Christmas with my family,' she said. 'Let me know the guest list and I'll send the invites out for you tomorrow.'

'Hang on. This is going way too fast for me, Sophie,' he said, panic flooding through him at the idea.

'OK. I'll back off. Maybe not a big gathering at your house this year. But you still need to invite both the grannies to the nursery school Christmas concert. And Cindy. *And* me, even though I'll be officially not needed by then.'

Jamie rather thought he'd still be needing her. But he didn't know how to tell her. So instead he said, 'My turn to be bossy. Come and have lunch with me on Wednesday.'

'Since when do you have a lunch break?'

'You had lunch with me when we talked about a temporary transfer for Georgia and Lily,' he pointed out.

'So this is a business lunch?'

'Personal,' he said.

She smiled, and butterflies started dancing in her stomach. 'I still think this is a bad idea. But OK. It's a…'

'It's a date,' he said softly. He drew her hand up to his mouth and pressed a kiss in the palm. 'You and me. I'll pick you up from your office. You can tell everyone it's business, if you like. But I'm telling you now there will be hand-holding involved. And I intend to make sure there's some mistletoe around.'

'Like this?' She sketched some in the air with her fingertip.

What else could he do but kiss her?

And she was gratifyingly flushed by the time he broke the kiss. 'Well, Ms Firth.'

'Well, Mr Wallis.' Her voice was gratifyingly husky, too.

'Oh, and while I remember—I can't come over to look after Sienna tomorrow.'

He frowned. 'Why not?'

'I have a small problem. To be more accurate, a small four-footed and waggy-tailed problem,' she said.

He blinked. 'You have a dog?' Yet she'd never mentioned a pet before.

'Just for tomorrow,' she explained. 'I'm puppy-sitting for my friend so she can do her Christmas shopping—so if you need me to look after Sienna you're going to have to bring her to my place.' She paused. 'You can work there, if you like. My kitchen table functions very well as a desk.'

It sounded seriously domestic. Something that should have had him running for cover. But the idea was too irresistible to turn down. 'OK.'

'And Mandy was asking if Sienna can come for lunch and play with Hattie on Sunday afternoon.'

Given that Sophie was being so accommodating, he thought that he really ought to do the same. 'Sure.'

'Great.' She stole another kiss. 'Right. We both have work to do. See you tomorrow.'

'Tomorrow.' And he was really looking forward to it.

On Saturday, at Sophie's flat, Jamie felt as if he'd just stepped into a hug. The place was warm and comfortable, and she had photographs everywhere. The mantelpiece was full of graduation and wedding photographs, plus pictures of children he assumed were Hattie and Sam, and a picture of her and Eva at the Eiffel Tower. There were hand-drawn cards on the mantelpiece, and childish art-work held to the outside of her fridge with magnets.

Sophie Firth was clearly much loved. And he could see why.

'Meet Archie,' she said.

The liver and white springer spaniel wrig-gled in her arms, clearly desperate to get down and start bouncing about.

'Are you ready for this, Sienna? He's very lively. And very lovely,' she said with a smile.

'Yay!' Sienna said.

Sophie knelt on the floor and let the pup down. He bounced about, his tail a wagging blur and his soft paws scrabbling everywhere, then leapt onto Sienna's lap and proceeded to wash her face with his tongue, much to her joy.

'I love him!' Sienna said.

'He'll calm down in a minute. Libby, my friend who owns him, says he does tricks. Shall we see if he'll do them for us?'

Sienna nodded and cuddled the puppy.

'Coffee?' Sophie said to Jamie.

'I'll make it.'

She shook her head. 'Get yourself settled

at the table. I don't have a posh coffee maker like yours, but I promise it's decent coffee.'

She made coffee for them and poured a glass of milk for Sienna; although Jamie was officially supposed to be working at his laptop, he couldn't help watching Sophie as she showed Sienna how to get Archie to sit and hold up one paw for treats.

It wasn't that maybe he could fall in love with Sophie Firth.

He already had.

That innate warmth and kindness, the sweetness of her mouth—she was adorable. Even when she was being bossy, it wasn't like the way his mother took over things; she had a way of making it feel as if you'd been the one to make the suggestion in the first place.

And there was a strong bond between Sophie and his daughter.

For the first time in two years, he could see the future—and he liked what he saw. A future full of laughter and love and real happiness.

He knew he didn't deserve it.

But for Sienna's sake—and Sophie's—he'd work for it.

Sophie and Sienna took the pup out for a walk, once Sophie had finished her milk. 'We can only take him out for a little while,'

Sophie explained, 'because he's still a baby. Libby says it's five minutes' walk for each month of the pup's age, so that's fifteen minutes of walking and I'll have to carry him after that.'

'Will you come with us, Daddy?' Sienna asked.

He was supposed to be working.

But the sun was shining. How could he resist his daughter's entreaties—or the big amber eyes of the spaniel? 'Sure,' he said. And Sophie's smile made him feel warm all over.

In the end, he was the one who ended up carrying the pup—who'd curled up and gone to sleep next to the park bench while Sienna was playing on the swings —and Sophie held Sienna's hand as the little girl skipped back to Sophie's flat.

Sophie made toasted cheese and ham sandwiches for lunch, and Archie had a tiny piece of ham along with his kibble, sitting nicely and putting his paw up to ask for a treat.

How could Jamie be anything but charmed?

Even when the pup had a couple of accidents on the kitchen floor by the back door, Sophie was good-natured about it. 'He's just a baby. And my kitchen floor isn't carpet. All

I need is a mop and some disinfectant. The floor'll dry quickly enough.'

Later in the afternoon, when Sienna had talked Jamie into watching a princess movie in the living room with them, the pup was quiet and Jamie assumed he'd fallen asleep next to Sophie's feet. But then Sophie went into the kitchen to make a drink and came back looking absolutely horrified.

'What's the matter?' he asked.

'You know all those memes where they say silence is golden—unless you have a pup, in which case silence is really, really suspicious?'

No, he didn't. He wasn't quite sure what a meme was, but the whole thing about a quiet pup being suspicious sounded like a warning. 'What's he done?'

'Your shoe,' Sophie said, looking guilty, and handed it to him. 'He's chewed it. Um, quite badly.'

Both ends of the lace had been bitten off to the point where it was unusable, and the pup had chewed all round the inner edge of the shoe. The tongue beneath the laces was particularly badly savaged. No way was he going to be able to repair them.

'I should've kept a closer eye on him,' she said, biting her lip.

'Hey—I was here, too,' he said. 'I thought he was asleep. It isn't your fault.'

'Are you going to be able to drive home?'

'If you can lend me a lace to keep me going,' he said. 'But I don't think I'll be wearing those shoes again after that.'

'I'll replace them.'

He shook his head. 'It's fine. And it's a good lesson to learn: never leave shoes around within a puppy's reach.'

Sophie carried the dog over to a cupboard in the living room and searched one-handed in a drawer. 'I don't have any laces,' she said. 'But I think I can do something with elastic bands.'

'Thanks,' he said.

When the film ended, he said, 'We need to go home now, Sienna.'

The little girl shook her head. 'I want to stay with Sophie and Archie.'

'Not today,' he said. 'We can maybe come and visit another time.'

'But Archie won't be here.' Her lower lip wobbled.

'Maybe we can go and see him together at my friend Libby's house, another day,' Sophie suggested.

'Can we, Daddy?' Sienna asked. 'Please?'

'Yes, darling. But we need to let Sophie get on.'

'Bye, Sophie.' The little girl hugged her. 'Thank you for having me. Love you.'

Sophie hugged her back. 'It was a pleasure and I love you, too.'

Archie, not to be outdone, licked Sienna's face.

'And I love you, too, Archie.' Sienna kissed the pup's nose.

'I'll see you tomorrow afternoon, just after lunch, and we'll go and play with Hattie,' Sophie said. 'I'll just fix Daddy's shoe before you go.'

She did something complicated with the elastic bands, and to his surprise they actually held his shoe on his foot.

'I really am sorry about the shoes,' she said.

'It's fine. It's not as if they were brand new.' He smiled at her. 'See you tomorrow. And thank you for today. It's been great.' It shocked him how much he'd enjoyed it. Even though Sophie's flat was tiny, it was warm and welcoming and he'd felt completely at home.

This was all going way too fast. Scarily so.

But he didn't think he wanted to stop it.

CHAPTER SEVEN

SOPHIE WAS HALFWAY to Mandy's house with Sienna in the car seat on Sunday when her phone rang. She switched it through to the hands-free system on the car. 'Hello?'

'Soph, it's Mandy. Sorry, I meant to ring you earlier. Sam's gone down with a rotten cold and he's running a temperature.'

'Ah. So we need to reschedule the play date?' Sophie asked.

'Sort of,' Mandy said. 'Will's going to look after Sam for me. I thought maybe we could take the girls swimming instead.'

'Hang on a tick. Would you like to go swimming, Sienna?' Sophie asked.

'I've never been swimming,' the little girl said.

Sophie glanced at her in surprise. Given that Jamie owned several resorts, all of which had a pool... Surely he'd visited them with Sienna and let her enjoy the children's activities?

'Sienna's the same size as Hattie and she's got two costumes, so Sienna can borrow one,' Mandy said. 'And you can borrow a costume from me, Sophie. We've got spare swimming towels and spare armbands, too. Would you like to go swimming, Sienna?'

'Yes, please!' Sienna said, and it was settled.

At Mandy's house, they moved Sienna's car seat to the back and fixed Hattie's next to it, and the two little girls chattered all the way to the sports centre.

But Sienna clung to Sophie's hand on the way from the changing rooms to the pool, clearly nervous.

'It'll be fine, Sienna,' Sophie reassured her. 'We're going in the little pool, and it isn't very deep. I promise I won't let you go under the water. We're just going to sit and play.'

It took a little while for Sienna to relax, but once she'd overcome her initial nervousness of the water she started copying Hattie, the two little girls had a wonderful time in the pool.

'This is the perfect Sunday afternoon,' Mandy said with a smile, and Sophie had to agree.

Jamie glanced at his watch. It was nearly four in the afternoon and it was starting to get dark. Plus it had been raining steadily for the last hour, so they couldn't have been at the park. Surely Sophie should have brought Sienna back by now?

Feeling twitchy, he was about to call Sophie's mobile phone when he heard the sound of car tyres on gravel.

Sienna rushed to find him as soon as the front door opened. 'Daddy, Daddy, guess what? Me and Hattie went swimming!'

It felt as if his blood was roaring through his ears.

Swimming.

Fran had died, swimming. She'd died in the ocean and he hadn't been with her. Guilt slammed into him. And the woman he'd been considering bringing into his life, into Fran's place, *had taken his daughter swimming.*

She'd really overstepped the mark—and so had he.

He wasn't going to yell at her in front of Sienna. But he couldn't just let this go.

'Darling, can you go upstairs and draw me a picture?' he asked once he'd greeted his daughter with a kiss.

'Yes, Daddy.' Sienna beamed at him and skipped up the stairs.

'Kitchen. Now,' he mouthed at Sophie.

She frowned, but followed him in there.

'Close the door,' he said, his voice clipped.

Her frown deepened. 'Jamie? What's going on?'

'I need to talk to you and I don't want Sienna to hear any of this,' he said, keeping his voice low.

She closed the door. 'I don't understand. What's the problem?'

'You took Sienna swimming.'

'Because Sam had a rotten cold and Mandy didn't want Sienna to pick it up. She called me when I was about halfway to their house and suggested we could go swimming instead. Sienna said she'd love to go when we asked her, so Mandy lent us both costumes and towels plus some armbands for Sienna.'

'You took Sienna swimming,' he repeated.

'Which is a perfectly normal thing to do with a small child,' Sophie protested. 'The pool's not far from Mandy's house, there are lifeguards, and actually there's a very shallow pool especially for little ones, so she wasn't in any danger of teenagers splashing her or bumping into her by accident.'

She really wasn't listening. Did he have to tell her in words of one syllable? 'I don't want her swimming, and you had no right to take her without asking.'

'You left her in my charge,' she reminded

him. 'You were in a meeting, so I didn't get the chance to ask your permission. And I don't see why swimming is such a big problem for you. It's a life skill Sienna's going to need when she's older and she'll have swimming lessons at junior school, so it's a good idea to start getting her used to the water now.'

He clenched his teeth. 'Fran died because she went swimming.'

Sophie stared at him as his words sank in, her face paling with shock. 'Fran *drowned*? Oh, my God. I'm so sorry, Jamie. I had no idea. I thought she died because she fell ill while you were abroad.'

'She didn't drown,' Jamie corrected. 'She went diving and got scratched on a coral reef. It turned out she was allergic to the coral sting—she went into anaphylactic shock. The diver with her called for help and started bringing her back to shore, but the allergic reaction made her face and throat swell up, she couldn't breathe and her heart stopped. She was dead by the time the medics got to them.'

'I'm so sorry. I didn't know.' Sophie blew out a breath. 'Why didn't you tell me?'

'It's not exactly the kind of thing that comes up in conversation.'

'But you could have made sure the information was in Cindy's file. What if the real temporary nanny had taken Sienna swimming?'

'Swimming isn't on the list of activities Sienna does. The real temporary nanny,' he pointed out, 'would have stuck to the rules.' Whereas Sophie had well and truly broken them.

'Jamie, I don't know what to say. I'm sorry. But what are you going to do when Sienna goes to school? Tell her teacher that she's the only child in the class who's not allowed to go swimming?'

'Yes,' he said.

The expression of anguish in her eyes turned to anger. 'That's not reasonable, and you know it. What happened to Fran was desperately tragic, and I'm sorry for your loss and Sienna's, but there aren't any coral reefs in English indoor swimming pools. And what if when Sienna's older and she's messing about with a group of friends, and one of them thinks it'd be funny to throw her into an outdoor pool? If she can't swim and it's a deep pool, what then? You're prepared to let her drown?'

'Her friends will be too sensible to throw her in a pool.'

She rolled her eyes. 'Jamie, you were a teenager yourself once. A student. You know how sometimes things get out of hand. Nobody means any harm, but things happen. Isn't it better that she knows how to get out of trouble?'

'My daughter doesn't swim. End of,' he said curtly. He couldn't tolerate the idea.

'But—'

'No buts,' he cut in.

'You're not being fair to her.'

'I don't care. She doesn't swim.'

Sophie blew out a breath. 'So, what? You're never going to take her to the seaside, either?'

'Correct.' How could he let her anywhere near the sea, the thing that had killed her mother? Why couldn't Sophie understand that he was trying to protect his little girl? 'That's one of the reasons we don't go to Norfolk. Do you know where Fran's parents live? In a village right next to the North Sea.' It was way, way too dangerous.

'Why?' she asked, shaking her head in apparent confusion. 'Why are you going to deprive Sienna of the sheer joy of paddling at the edge of the sea on a hot summer's day, when you know she'll be perfectly safe because you're holding your hand? Why won't you let her build a sandcastle, put seaweed flags and shells on the towers, and fill up the moat with sea water? Why won't you let her look for foss—?' She broke off. 'Hang on. I told you about my childhood, about me and my brothers wanting to find a dinosaur on the beach at Lyme Regis. You could've said something then.'

'Sienna was with us.'

'Later, then,' she said. 'Why didn't you tell me?'

'Because it was all my fault!' The words came out slightly louder than he'd intended, and she flinched.

But she didn't back down.

She didn't stop asking questions, either.

'Why was it your fault, Jamie?'

'Because it should've been me,' he said. 'We were in the Caribbean, looking at a potential new resort. The place looked fine and we planned to try out the activities on offer. I was meant to go out diving around the coral reef, but I'd eaten something that disagreed with me and was ill that morning, so she went out instead. And she died.' He clenched his teeth. 'None of us knew she was allergic to coral. If I hadn't been ill I would've been the one who was stung, not her. It would've been painful, maybe. But Fran would still be alive.'

* * *

Sophie had assumed that Fran had died from some kind of tropical disease—but now she knew Fran's death had been caused by an allergic reaction to a coral sting, and Jamie blamed himself because she'd taken his place on the diving trip when he'd been too sick to go.

Now she understood why he was being so unreasonable about her taking Sienna swimming. And why he'd backed away from his daughter, not just because she reminded him of what he'd lost, but she reminded him of his guilt.

Guilt he shouldn't been carrying in the first place, because it hadn't been his fault at all.

'You might have been allergic to the coral, too,' she pointed out.

'I'm not.'

'It's not your fault that Fran died.'

He gave her a look of sheer contempt. 'Of course it is. If I'd gone on the diving trip instead of her, she wouldn't have been scratched by the coral and she wouldn't have died.'

'You'd eaten something that disagreed with you,' she reminded. 'In that situation, when you're being sick or you've got an upset stomach, you can't even walk round a resort, let alone anything else. You need to rest and stay close to a bathroom and drink plenty of water. Diving was completely out of the question.'

'It's my fault,' he repeated stubbornly.

'No. But I tell you what *is* your fault,' she said. 'Sienna and Rose. You're backing away from them because every time you see them they remind you of Fran, and you feel the loss and the guilt all over again.' She lifted her chin. 'For their sake, you have to break the cycle and get past it. Don't let it ruin Sienna's life any more than it has already. Find a counsellor who can help you.'

'It has nothing to do with you,' he said.

'Actually, as I'm her temporary nanny, it has everything to do with me,' she said.

No, it didn't. He couldn't handle this. What the hell had he been thinking? He was better off as he'd been before he'd met Sophie. Alone. *Safe*.

He knew what he needed to do now. 'That's easily sorted.' He stared at her. 'I'll call the agency tomorrow morning and ask them to send someone. You've been here a month. At least some of their staff must've recovered from that virus by now.'

'What?' She looked at him in disbelief. 'You can't sack me. You're not my boss.'

'I believe the phrase you used is "a business partner who doesn't interfere".' He folded his arms and glared at her. 'I'm not interfering in Plans & Planes, and you're not interfering with my life any more.'

'Don't be so ridiculous. I'm not interfering.' She shook her head, trying to clear it. 'I'm trying to understand what the hell's going on in your head.'

'You don't need to. Now, I'd like my car key and front door key back, please.' He held out his hand.

'You don't mean this.' He couldn't mean this. She could just about handle the fact that he wanted to keep the relationship between the two of them strictly business—all along she'd expected this to be third time unlucky—but he *couldn't* take it out on Sienna. Not like this. 'The deal is that I'm looking after Sienna until Cindy's leg is healed.'

He lifted a shoulder. 'I've changed my mind. I'd like you to go. Now.'

'Then do I at least get to say goodbye to Sienna?'

'I don't think that's appropriate.'

What? Sophie could understand why he was upset—her actions had inadvertently brought back his loss and grief—but this was totally unreasonable. 'That's not fair. She's lost enough in her life.'

He gave her another of those witheringly cold looks. 'You should've thought about that before you took her swimming.'

'Oh, for pity's sake! *I didn't know how Fran died*,' she reminded him through clenched teeth.

'Even if you had, would it have made a difference?'

'Yes. Of course it would. I would've discussed it with you.'

His expression said that he didn't believe her. 'My keys.'

Right now he wasn't being reasonable; the more she argued with him, the more entrenched he was becoming. So maybe it was better to give a little ground now and try to talk about it again when he'd calmed down. She rummaged in her bag and took out the keys. 'Please don't do this, Jamie. It's not fair on any of us.'

'Thank you for your help over the last month,' he said coolly.

Help? It wasn't just helping him out over a childcare crisis. It had started out that way, yes—but they'd grown close over the last few weeks. He'd been trying to persuade her to date him. They'd kissed. Held each other.

And now he was ending it.

Ending everything.

'Tell Sienna if she ever needs anything, I'm here,' she said.

'That won't be necessary,' Jamie said, and his expression was practically Arctic.

Maybe tomorrow, when he'd calmed down a bit, she could try talking to him again. But for now she concentrated on putting one foot in front of the other, and walked out of the kitchen. Out of his house. Out of his life.

Jamie watched the door close behind Sophie. He couldn't believe how quickly and how badly the row had escalated.

Why did he feel that this was somehow his fault? Because it wasn't. Sophie had taken Sienna swimming without asking him. How could Sophie not see that she was massively in the wrong?

He damped down the hurt and anger and frustration, not wanting Sienna to see it, and went to check on her.

'Where's Sophie?' she asked, looking up from her drawing.

'She had to go.'

'But she didn't come and kiss me goodbye.' Sienna's bottom lip wobbled.

'She had to go to a meeting,' Jamie fibbed,

hating himself for lying but wanting to save his daughter from any more hurt.

'Oh. Well, I'll give her my picture tomorrow,' she said.

Sophie wasn't going to be there tomorrow. Not that he was going to tell Sienna that right now. And guilt squeezed him even harder when he saw what she'd drawn: a swimming pool, with two little girls who were clearly herself and Hattie, and two women who were clearly Sophie and Hattie's mum.

Sienna had obviously loved her afternoon at the swimming pool.

And he hated himself that little bit more.

'But why isn't Sophie taking me to nursery school?' Sienna wailed the next morning when Jamie broke the news to her. 'I need to give her my picture!'

'Sophie can't look after you any more,' Jamie said. 'I'm sorry.'

'Is that because she's in heaven with Mummy?'

The question cut him to the quick. Was that really the first thing his daughter thought of when someone was no longer around? Sophie had suggested it but he hadn't really believed her. Now he was beginning to think that Sophie might've been right. 'No, she's not in heaven, darling. She's just busy at work. She was only helping out as long as she could until Cindy's better.'

Sienna was crying. 'I love Sophie.'

So do I, Jamie thought, but she put you at risk and I can't handle that. And I can't handle feeling things that I can't control, either. 'I'm going to take you to nursery school this morning. You'll have a new nanny this afternoon who'll look after you until Cindy's leg is mended.'

And Ellen turned out to be everything he wanted in a nanny. Middle-aged, no-nonsense, and she stuck to the rules in the file.

Though he did keep two things from Sophie's regime. He ate dinner with Sienna, even though Ellen kept to the nursery menus rather than the kind of food Sophie had let Sienna help her cook. And he made sure that he was the one to read Sienna a bedtime story. Tough, since the swimming incident, Ellen was the one who did bathtimes and hairwashing.

'Right,' Eva said on Wednesday morning, perching on the edge of Sophie's desk. 'Ignore all your calls. We need to talk. What's happened?'

'It doesn't matter,' Sophie said, looking away.

Eva raised her eyebrows. 'On Monday, you looked as if you'd cried yourself to sleep the previous night, then cried all through your shower that morning.'

She had.

'Yesterday, you looked twice as bad. Today, you look worse still. So something's obviously up, Soph. And, yes, I know I'm going away soon, but I'm still your best friend and I'll always be here for you. So *talk* to me.'

'Sorry.' Sophie scrubbed at her eyes. 'Give me a tick and I'll sort out my make-up a bit better.'

Eva reached across the desk and hugged her. 'I'd much rather you talked to me.'

'All right.' Sophie blew out a breath. 'Jamie sacked me.'

Eva stared at her in obvious disbelief. 'What?'

'As Sienna's nanny.'

'Why?'

'I took her swimming.' Sophie bit her lip. 'I thought you said Fran died from an unexpected illness.'

'She did,' Eva said.

'Jamie told me she went diving and had a massive allergic reaction to a scratch on coral,' Sophie said. 'He went bananas when he realised I'd taken Sienna swimming.'

'Oh, my God. I had no idea that's what her illness was. I just assumed...' Eva spread her hands, looking upset. 'Well. It didn't feel right to ask for details. We all just assumed it was some tropical disease that didn't have a cure.' Eva hugged Sophie again. 'He'll calm down and apologise.'

'It doesn't matter about an apology. I just want him to calm down and for things to be back to how they were.' Sophie squeezed her eyes shut. 'He's not answering any of my calls, Eva.'

'He's got a Y chromosome,' Eva reminded her. 'It means he doesn't always think things through.'

'I miss Sienna.'

Eva gave her a narrow look. 'And you miss Jamie. It wasn't just business, was it?'

'You know my track record in men. I always pick Mr Wrong.' Sophie sighed heavily. 'I screwed up yet again.'

'Jamie's a nice guy. He's fair—well, most of the time he's fair,' Eva amended. 'Just give him a chance to calm down. Then he'll realise he's been a total idiot. He won't know how to fix things, being a guy, but give him a few more days and then try calling him again, act as if nothing's happened, and...'

Sophie shook her head. 'It's over, Eva. I blew it.'

Eva hugged her again. 'I'll talk to him.'

'No. I don't want to be the pathetic woman who doesn't know when to stop and drags everyone else into the break-up,' Sophie said. 'I just have to chalk this down to experience.' And she was never, ever going to let herself lose her heart to anyone again.

Order. That was what Jamie liked. What Ellen was making sure he had.

So why did it feel so wrong? he wondered.

No more home-made Christmas decorations; but he hadn't removed the tree that he'd decorated with Sienna and Sophie, hideously garish and tacky though it was.

No more Sienna trotting into his office to interrupt him, with flour smeared across her face and in her hair, carrying a cookie or a cupcake she'd baked especially for him and looking so pleased with herself.

No more chaos or dancing or singing.

And it got worse on Saturday when he and Sienna queued up to see Santa at the grotto in a nearby department store. There was tinnily annoying Christmas music, teenagers capering about dressed as elves, children in the queue getting fretful because the wait to see Santa was getting too much for them...

If Sophie had been with them, it would've been different. She would've got the kids around them singing along with the Christmas songs and doing the traditional actions. She would've revelled in the spirit of things; whereas Jamie felt distinctly Scrooge-like and had to bite his tongue to stop himself saying, 'Bah, humbug!'

He missed Sophie.

Irrationally and stupidly, he missed her. He missed the warmth of her smile, the laughter in her eyes, the way she made a room feel like home just by walking into it.

And he didn't have a clue what to say to his daughter to get them through the interminable wait to see Santa. Sophie would probably have spun some story about the elves in Santa's workshop to distract the little girl. But he didn't have the words. He wouldn't even know where to start. And Sienna was just clinging to his hand, white-faced, looking as if she wanted to be a million miles away.

He could do with being a million miles away from all this nonsense, too.

He'd even suggested that morning that maybe they should skip the visit, but Sienna had been stubborn about it. 'Sophie said we were going to see Santa.'

So Santa it was.

And his own Christmas spirit had more than deserted him, Jamie thought grimly.

Finally they were at the head of the queue, and Santa gave a jolly laugh as they walked in. 'Good morning, young lady. And what's your name?'

'Sienna,' she said shyly.

'That's a lovely name. And you've come out all the way to see me today?'

She nodded.

'I'm very pleased. Have you been a good girl?'

'Yes,' she whispered.

'I know you wrote to me to tell me, but I always like to hear children tell me. So what would you like for Christmas, Sienna?' he asked.

She took a deep breath. 'I want Sophie to be my new mummy.'

'Well, sweetheart, that's a bit tricky, because the presents I give are all wrapped up, and I can't wrap a person up,' Santa said gently.

'Daddy had a big fight with Sophie and she went away,' Sienna said.

Jamie wanted the earth to open up and swallow him.

'I love Sophie, and she loves me.' Sienna's bottom lip began to wobble and a tear rolled down her cheek. 'I want her to be my mummy. My mummy's in heaven but Sophie isn't. And I love Sophie.'

Jamie dropped to his knees beside her and put his arms round her. 'Don't cry, darling. And I don't think Santa has time to talk about this right now.'

'Oh, Santa *always* has time,' Santa corrected, giving him a speaking look, and Jamie felt about two centimetres tall. 'Tell me about Sophie, Sienna.'

'She came to look after me when Cindy, my nanny, broke her leg. Sophie's lovely. I love Sophie. My grannies love Sophie.' Sophie swallowed a sob. '*Everybody* loves Sophie.'

'Does Daddy love Sophie?' Santa asked gently.

'I don't know. But I think Sophie loves Daddy.'

How? Jamie wondered. How could Sophie possibly love him, when it was his fault that Sienna's mother was dead, he was a rubbish father, and he'd pushed Sophie away without letting her have a say?

'I think,' Santa said, 'you and Daddy need to talk. And sometimes it's hard to say the right words, so I'm going to give you a very special teddy bear to help you. A black and white teddy bear.'

'Like a penguin?' Sienna asked.

He smiled. 'Just like a penguin. What you do is sit with Daddy and you tell the teddy bear what you want to say to Daddy. And then things will work out. I can't give you a mummy for Christmas, sweetheart, but that bear will help you.'

'Thank you.' Sienna accepted the wrapped present gratefully. 'Thank you, Santa.'

'Merry Christmas,' he said.

'Merry Christmas,' Jamie said. 'And thank you.'

Sienna clutched the bear tightly as they left Santa's grotto.

'Would you like to go for a milkshake?' he asked.

She shook her head.

He had a pretty good idea what his daughter wanted to do instead. 'Let's go home and talk to the bear,' he said. 'Though maybe we should get him a Christmas hat first.' Because that was what he was pretty sure Sophie would've suggested.

They bought the Christmas hat for the bear and headed back to their house. Ellen was there, waiting for them; she smiled and was kind, but she just wasn't Sophie. And the house wasn't home without Sophie, either.

They ate lunch, though Sienna didn't eat much, pushing her food around on the plate because she was clearly too upset to eat. Then, finally, they sat down with the bear. Jamie knew that this was going to test him to his limits; and he also knew that, whatever happened, he was not going to let his little girl down.

'Why did Daddy fight with Sophie, Bear?' Sienna asked.

'Because sometimes Daddy gets things wrong, and Daddy needs to learn to listen,' he said.

Sienna looked thoughtful. 'Does Daddy love Sophie like I do, Bear?'

He owed her honesty. 'Yes, I do.'

She turned to him, the bear temporarily forgotten. 'So can Sophie be my mummy?'

That was the key question. The one he couldn't answer without Sophie.

'It's not just up to me, darling,' he said. 'I need to talk to Sophie. And you know sometimes when you have a fight with a friend, it takes a little while to make things up?'

She nodded solemnly.

'I promise I'll try to make things up with her. But it might take a while.' He paused.

'Would you like to draw a picture of your bear?'

'For Sophie?'

He nodded. If need be, he could always photograph it on his phone and text it to Sophie—or maybe ask Eva to play postman for him, if Sophie was ignoring him.

When Sienna was settled, he took his phone, ready to text Sophie.

Where did he start?

They'd both been in the wrong. But saying that was maybe not the most tactful opening.

In the end, he sent the simplest message he could think of.

Please can we talk?

If she ignored him or said no, he'd have to try a different approach. But the most important thing right now was re-establishing contact.

There was no answer. She might be busy, he told himself. Her phone might be stuffed in her handbag, in a different room, and she might not have heard it signal an incoming message or seen the text.

Or she might do what he'd done when she'd tried to call him earlier in the week and just ignore the message.

He hoped, for all their sakes, her silence was just because she was busy.

'Ellen, would you mind looking after Sienna for a few minutes for me, please?' he asked.

'Of course I will, Mr Wallis,' she said.

'Are you going to see Sophie?' Sienna asked hopefully.

'Not yet,' he said. 'I need to wait for her to answer my text first.'

She looked deflated. 'You're going to work.'

No, but he didn't want to burden her with where he was going. 'Yes,' he fibbed. 'I'll be as quick as I can.'

He grabbed his coat and headed to the florist round the corner to buy flowers, then walked to the cemetery.

Suitably, it was raining.

He took out the old flowers from the vase on Fran's grave and put the new ones in their place. 'Hi,' he said. 'I miss you.'

And of course she didn't answer. She couldn't answer.

'I'm sorry,' he said. 'I let you down. If I hadn't eaten that stupid fish curry, I wouldn't have been ill and it would've been me scratching myself on the coral reef, not you. You would still have been here to see our daughter grow up.'

And he'd let her down there, too. He swallowed hard.

'I've made a real mess of it, Fran. I've been a coward and an idiot, and I've hurt Sienna. I've hurt your mum. I've behaved like *my* mum.'

The rain came down a little bit harder.

'I want to make it right,' he said. 'With Sophie, I was getting there. She showed me how to be a proper dad to Sienna. How to be human again instead of a block of ice.' He sighed. 'Except I overreacted and I pushed her away.'

And he didn't know if she was going to give him a second chance. He didn't deserve one, not for his own sake. But surely Sienna deserved a chance?

'I love you,' he said to Fran, 'and I always will. But Sienna's growing up and she really needs a mum. And I need someone to—well, manage me, I guess. Someone I can love, the way I love you. Because love doesn't just fit in a little box. It expands.' He dragged in a breath. 'I want to be a family again. And it feels right with Sophie. It doesn't mean I don't love you any more. And I'll never forget you. I'll remember you every time I hear our daughter laugh. And I want to hear Sienna laugh a lot, Fran. I don't want her to grow up like I did, a kid who was seen but never heard. I want her to have a normal childhood. To feel loved. So I'm going to ask Sophie to forgive me, and I'll do whatever it takes to persuade her to give me a second chance—to marry me and be a family with me. I hope you can understand that.'

And maybe he was just being fanciful: but right at that moment the rain stopped, and a ray of sunlight caught the droplets of rain on the flowers he'd put in the vase in front of Fran's grave.

Was it Fran giving him a push and telling him that life had to go on, and she wanted him to find happiness?

He hoped so.

It certainly made his heart feel lighter.

He rested his hand on her grave. 'I love you, Fran. I'm sorry we didn't get the chance to grow old together. But I've met someone who's taught me to love again, someone who's taught me to reconnect with our daughter. And I hope we're going to have a happy life.' He swallowed hard. 'I just need to get her to forgive me, first.'

Just.

Funny how he could negotiate difficult

contracts and do megabuck deals without turning a hair. But this emotional minefield… He just had to hope that Sophie would talk to him and give him the chance he'd been too stupid to give her.

CHAPTER EIGHT

Please can we talk?

SOPHIE STARED AT the screen. Given that Jamie had ignored her phone calls last week and had made it very clear that he didn't want anything to do with her, this was the last thing she'd expected—to the point where she'd left her phone in her handbag and hadn't bothered checking it, so the message had been sitting there unread for a couple of hours.

What did he want to talk to her about?

The fact he'd started with the word 'please' was a good thing; it sounded as if he really was prepared to discuss things instead of going off at the deep end. And she'd been so miserable without him and Sophie in her life. Even throwing herself into work hadn't helped much; she was too aware of how much she missed them.

OK.

Monday, half-past twelve?

That question mark made all the difference: it meant this was a suggestion, not a demand.

Fine. Suggest somewhere neutral?

The café opposite your office? Or do you know somewhere better?

Café's fine. See you at twelve-thirty.

See you then.

Sophie found it really hard to concentrate at work on Monday.

'You're twitchy,' Eva said.

'Because I'm meeting Jamie at lunchtime,' Sophie admitted. 'He wants to talk.'

Eva smiled. 'See? Told you so. All he needed was some time to calm down.'

'Maybe. But I have absolutely no idea what he wants to talk about.'

'He's probably working out how to apologise because he knows he's in the wrong,' Eva said. 'Do you want me to come with you?'

'I love you dearly for offering,' Sophie said, 'but it's fine.'

'Where are you meeting him?'

'At the café across the road from here.'

'Then text me if you need me and I'll be straight over,' Eva said.

'I will.' Sophie hugged her. 'Thank you.'

She walked into the café at twenty-nine minutes past twelve. Jamie was already there, and was sitting at a table where she could see him easily from the door. He raised a hand as she scanned the room. That tiny hint of vulnerability in his smile melted her heart.

But he probably wanted to discuss business, she warned herself. This wasn't going to be personal. Maybe he wanted her to talk to the new nanny about some of the things she'd done with Sienna. So she wasn't going to let herself remember how it had felt when he'd held her hand and kissed her. That was in the past and it was staying there.

She walked over to him. 'Hello, Jamie.'

'Thank you for coming, Sophie,' he said. 'Can I get you some coffee?'

'Thank you. That'd be nice.'

He gestured to the chair opposite his. 'Please sit down. I'll be back in a minute.'

Her nervousness increased as she waited. He'd still given her absolutely no idea what he wanted to talk to her about, and she couldn't tell a thing about his mood from his polite formality.

He returned bearing a mug of coffee just the way she liked it.

'Thank you,' she said.

'I'm glad you agreed to meet me.'

'Uh-huh.' She'd already decided to let him do most of the talking, so she waited to hear what he had to say.

'First of all,' he said, 'I owe you a massive apology—I went off at the deep end, last week, and I shouldn't have taken out my worries on you.'

She narrowed her eyes at him. 'Or sacked me, when you weren't technically my boss.'

'Or asked you to leave,' he said, 'when you'd done so much to make Sienna's life better—and mine.' He sighed. 'I'm an idiot.'

'I'd kind of already worked that one out for myself.' Her resolve to let him do all the talking vanished in a rush of curiosity. 'But what made you see it?'

'Would you believe, a stuffed panda?'

Sophie stared at him, not understanding. 'A stuffed panda? How?'

'I took Sienna to see Santa. He asked what she wanted for Christmas,' Jamie explained. 'And he said he couldn't do what she wanted, but he gave her a bear and said if she used it to talk to me I might be able to sort things out.'

That was amazing psychology on Santa's part, she thought. 'What did she ask for?'

He winced. 'There's no way to prepare you for this, so I'll tell you straight. Sienna wanted you to be her mummy.'

Sophie stared at him, completely floored by what he'd just told her. 'I don't know what to say.'

He lifted a shoulder in a resigned half-shrug. 'You don't have to say anything.'

'What did you say?' she asked.

'To Santa or the bear?'

'Both.'

'Thank you to Santa. And to the bear...' He raked a hand through his hair. 'That was one of the toughest conversations I've ever had. I said that it wasn't just up to me. That I needed to talk to you. And sometimes when you have a fight with a friend it takes a little while to make things up.'

'Good answer,' she said. 'You didn't make any promises you can't keep and you were honest with Sienna.' Though had she just compounded her past mistakes? Was this like Joe and Dan all over again and Jamie only wanted her for what she could do for him, not for herself? 'Is that why you're talking to me now?'

'For her sake? Partly,' he admitted. 'But also for mine. I've been doing a lot of thinking, the last few days. The house doesn't feel right without you.'

'In other words, you don't like your new temp nanny?' she asked wryly.

'Ellen's lovely and she's going to stay with us until Cindy's back,' he said. 'It's not that at all. It's *you*. I miss you.'

Could she trust him? Did he mean it? She'd been here before.

Though Jamie wasn't Dan or Joe. It wasn't fair to judge him by her past mistakes.

'The last month, things have been different,' he said. 'You made me look at my life and I didn't like what I saw. And then I panicked when I found you'd taken Sienna swimming.' He took a deep breath. 'I'll be honest with you. Feelings make me twitchy. I like being in control. Emotions—well, I was panicking and refusing to admit things to myself, and I guess I used the swimming as an excuse to push you away. Which was unfair of me and wrong.'

And it had hurt her deeply.

'I like the person I am when I'm with you,' he said, 'and I want to keep being that person. I want you back in my life, Sophie, but not as Sienna's nanny and not just as my business partner.'

She didn't quite dare to hope. 'So what are you saying?'

'I know I messed up, and I know you've been hurt before—but I'd never cheat on you like Dan and Joe did, and I won't ever lie to you like they did.' He looked earnestly at her. 'Just as you've shown me that I can be a better person, I want to show you that you can trust me.'

'How do I know you won't go off at the deep end again, the next time I do or say something you don't like and I can't read your mind?' she asked.

'Because,' he said, 'you've taught me to talk. You and the bear that Santa gave Sienna. Plus you were right about the counselling. I talked to a friend who trained as a GP, and he recommended someone who happens to have a cancellation this week. So I'm going for the first session tomorrow.' His eyes narrowed for a moment. 'That Santa isn't related to you, by any chance, is he?'

'No. I have no idea who that particular Santa was, but I've arranged having a Santa at events before now, so I know the kind of training they do,' she explained. 'They're taught how to deal with it when small children ask them to make a terminally ill person better or bring someone back from heaven.'

'Or ask them if someone will be their mummy,' he added, wincing.

She nodded. 'And the way your Santa handled the situation sounds perfect.' Particularly as it had made Jamie sit down with his daughter and really communicate with her.

'So will you give me a chance to make it up to you and see how this thing works out between us?' he asked.

'No promises to Sienna,' she warned. Just in case it went wrong again.

'No promises,' he agreed. 'I just want to spend time with you. And I don't mean for Sienna's sake. For me, too. Dating you properly as well as spending family time with her.'

Dating you properly. A thrill went down her spine at the idea. 'OK. And it might be nice to meet your new nanny.'

He gave her a wry smile. 'Why do I get the feeling that you're going to tell her to ignore that file?'

'More than that, I'm going to rip that file into little pieces and jump up and down on it,' she said. 'And then I might put all the pieces in a puddle and jump up and down on them all over again.'

'I've kind of got the message,' he said.

'Good.'

'Will you come and have dinner with us tonight?'

'If you're cooking,' she said.

He nodded. 'Chicken parmigiana?'

'And banana penguins. You'll need Sienna's help for that.'

'Sounds good,' he said.

Then, to her shock, he leaned across the table and kissed her. His mouth was warm and sweet, and every nerve-end in her lips tingled.

'That wasn't part of the deal,' she said.

'It's how you're supposed to seal a deal,' he said.

'That's not how we sealed the deal about me being your temporary nanny and you buying out Eva.'

'And that was my mistake,' he said, and kissed her again. 'See you tonight. Six o'clock. And if you're late I'll serve you cold, congealed Brussels sprouts.'

She grinned. 'Sounds as if you're listening and learning.'

'I am.' His eyes were full of warmth. Full of promise.

And Sophie allowed herself just a tiny glimmer of hope for the future.

* * *

That evening, Sophie stood on Jamie's doorstep, clutching a bottle of wine and some chocolate Christmas tree decorations. How ridiculous to feel nervous. Jamie had asked her here, and she knew Sienna would be pleased to see her. All the same, she took a deep breath before she pressed the doorbell.

A few seconds later, the front door opened and Sienna rushed to greet her with a hug and a squeal. 'Sophie!'

'Hello, sweetheart.' She hugged the little girl. 'These are for you, to go on the tree.' If Jamie hadn't removed all the gaudy decorations and replaced them with subtle, tasteful, soulless ones.

'Thank you!'

'And this is for you,' she said, handing the wine to Jamie.

'Thank you.'

She laughed. 'You do know you've got chocolate smeared over your face, right?' And it was incredibly endearing, because it meant his attention had been completely on Sienna and making the banana penguins together, and he hadn't been thinking about mess.

He looked shocked. 'I have?'

'Uh-huh.' On impulse, she rubbed the smear away with her thumb.

His pupils widened, and she felt an answering lick of desire.

Had Sienna not been there, he might have greeted her very differently indeed. With a kiss, like the one he'd left her with in the café…

'Come in,' he said, and Sophie was gratified to hear the huskiness in his voice.

Dinner was fabulous. 'No sprouts,' he said with a grin. And she was really pleased to discover that he'd left the tree exactly as they'd decorated it together.

'Can I read your bedtime story tonight, Sienna?' she asked when she'd helped the little girl add the chocolate decorations to the tree.

'Yes, please,' Sienna said with a smile.

Sophie noticed that the black and white bear had pride of place on Sienna's pillow. The bear that had helped her break the final barriers with her father.

'Did Daddy ask you?' Sienna asked, when they were alone.

Sophie could guess exactly what Sienna was talking about. Would she be her new mummy? But it wasn't something she could answer yet. She and Jamie still needed to sort things out between them.

'He told me about Santa and how he talked to you and your lovely bear, here,' Sophie said. 'And you know when you have a big fight with someone, sometimes it takes a little while to make it up?'

Sienna nodded solemnly.

'That's where we are right now. Your dad and I still need to talk a bit more and finish making up. But one thing that won't ever change,' she promised, 'is me being part of your life. I'll always be there.'

Sienna hugged her. 'I love you.'

'I love you, too.' She read the story and kissed the little girl goodnight, before heading back downstairs to Jamie.

'Will you stay and have a glass of wine with me?' he asked.

'Yes, but there's something I need to do first,' she said.

He laughed. 'I'm way ahead of you. Come with me.' He ushered her into the kitchen, opened the file that was lying on the kitchen table and ripped up the first page, then offered her the next page. 'Your turn.'

Between them they ripped up the entire contents of the file.

'There aren't any puddles tonight,' Jamie said, 'but I can improvise, if you like.'

'Just knowing all those rules are gone is enough,' she said with a smile.

He poured them both a glass of wine. 'Come and sit with me.'

And she discovered that he really did mean sitting with him, when he scooped her off the sofa and settled her on his lap.

'This,' he said softly. 'This is what's been missing from my life. You, close to me. And thank you for giving me a second chance. I'm not going to mess it up.' He stole a kiss. 'I'm tempted to ask you to stay tonight, but I know it's too soon.'

'It is,' she agreed.

'Will you let me take you to dinner on Wednesday—just the two of us?' he asked.

'You mean on a proper date?'

'A proper date,' he confirmed. 'Ellen will babysit.'

'I'd like that,' she said.

'Good.' He stole another kiss. 'So how's work going?'

'OK. We've got Eva's leaving do on Thursday, and we're all going to miss her horribly.' She stroked his face. 'You?'

'We're closing the deal on the next resort,' he said. 'It's a former manor house in the Cotswolds, and we're going to run some specialist cookery courses.'

'Sounds good,' she said. 'And I guess you can showcase local foods to go with it.'

'And we always feature work by local artists, which we sell without taking commission,' he said. 'That way we help the local economy, too.'

And somehow they ended up talking business and bouncing ideas off each other.

'So much for "no interference",' he said wryly.

She smiled. 'Maybe we need to renegotiate that bit. Brainstorming with someone who isn't quite as involved as you are is really useful.'

'So when are you launching the Weddings Abroad service?'

'After Christmas,' she said. 'I've got slots booked at a few wedding fairs, and I'm working on pieces for wedding magazines and websites.'

'Let me know if you need to borrow any staff.'

'Thanks. I will.' She stole a kiss. 'And I'd better go. Good luck with the counselling tomorrow. Call me if you need to talk.'

'Thanks.' He stroked her face.

'And I'll see you on Wednesday.'

'I'll pick you up at seven—although I'm not actually eating with Sienna, I can still be with her when she has her dinner,' he said.

'And I think she'll be pleased that I'm going out somewhere with you.'

'Sienna *and* her bear,' Sophie said with a smile.

Jamie could barely concentrate all day on Wednesday. He'd managed to book a quiet table for two in a really romantic restaurant in Covent Garden; and when he called for Sophie at seven, he did a double-take.

He'd first met the efficient businesswoman in her navy suit. Then he'd seen the softer side of Sophie, wearing jeans and a sweater and happy to do messy things with a child or take her to the park. And now he was seeing another side of her, in a little black dress and high heels with her hair in a sophisticated updo and red lipstick that he itched to kiss off her.

'You look stunning,' he said.

She inclined her head. 'Thank you. You don't scrub up too badly yourself.'

He held her hand all the way there in the back of the taxi. They walked hand in hand around the marketplace and enjoyed the Christmas lights and decorations.

'We have to bring Sienna here,' Sophie said, 'to see this reindeer—she'll love it.'

And Jamie loved the fact that Sophie

thought of his daughter, even though they were out on a date.

The restaurant was full of fairy lights, and he could see how much she liked the ambience. He did, too.

'It's my first date in a long time,' she said.

'Me, too,' he said. 'In fact, it's my first "first" date in more than a decade.'

'So what was your first date like with Fran?' she asked.

And he really appreciated the fact that Sophie didn't shy away from talking about his late wife. 'Typical student thing. We went to see this super-arty play. I don't think either of us worked out what was meant to be happening. And then this door on stage got stuck and the whole thing fell apart.' He smiled at the memory. 'We felt a bit guilty, but we sneaked out in the interval and went for a drink instead.'

'Sounds like fun. And I know the kind of play you mean.' She smiled. 'I've seen a few of those in my time, too.'

'I think I prefer the more commercial stuff,' he said.

'As a former English student, I ought to say I like the arty, impenetrable stuff best,' she said. 'But I agree with you. I like something with characters I can root for.'

'Maybe,' he said, 'we could go to the theatre.'

'I'd like that,' she said. 'But, as it's Christmas, I'd vote for the panto. With Sienna. And popcorn.'

'That sounds good, too.'

She reached over to squeeze his hand. 'You don't have to answer, but how did the counselling go yesterday?'

'It's early days,' he said. 'But I like the guy, he's easy to talk to, and he's given me a ton of homework to do before next week.'

'That sounds positive,' she said.

He nodded. 'It's not going to be an instant fix, but I want it to work so I'm going to put the effort in.' For her sake and Sienna's, as well as his own.

The rest of the evening went incredibly quickly, and Jamie was shocked by how late it was when he glanced at his watch. 'Sorry. That was really selfish of me, considering it's midweek and it's Eva's last day tomorrow.'

'It's fine,' Sophie said with a smile. 'I've really enjoyed tonight.'

And he really enjoyed taking her home and kissing her goodnight on the doorstep.

'Can you sneak off for a couple of hours on Friday lunchtime?' he asked. 'It's the nursery school concert and I know Sienna would love you to be there. Especially as you made her angel costume.'

'Did you ask the grannies?' she asked.

'Strictly speaking, we're only supposed to have two tickets per child for the concert,' he said. 'But I talked the nursery school manager into letting me have three extra tickets, in the circumstances.'

'The grannies and Cindy?' she asked.

'Absolutely.'

'Good. OK. I'll meet you there,' she said, and gave him a lingering kiss. 'Goodnight, Jamie. And thank you for tonight.'

He waited for her to go indoors and close the door, then headed for the tube.

And his heart felt lighter than it had in years.

On Friday, Jamie waited in the nursery school reception area with Cindy and the grannies. As he expected, Sophie turned up dead on time. She kissed him warmly, hugged Cindy, and then turned to the grannies. 'Gwen and Rose. It's so lovely to meet you properly.'

'And you,' Rose said, hugging her. 'My niece Eva has told me so much about you, I feel I already know you.'

'Jamie tells me nothing,' Gwen said, 'but

Sienna's said a lot.' She smiled, and hugged Sophie too.

No inquisition from my mother? Jamie thought, surprised. But it was a relief, too.

They found their seats and Jamie laced his fingers through Sophie's.

And the concert was magical.

Last year, he would've been wincing at the out of tune singing; this year, he found it charming. And, best of all, his little girl was standing on the stage in a white dress, with huge lacy angel wings trimmed in marabou and a headband with a marabou halo. Teamed with her golden curls, the effect was enough to make him have to blink back the tears.

Though he noticed there wasn't a dry eye in the house after 'Away in a Manger' and then 'Twinkle Twinkle'.

Christmas.

And this year was going to be a really, really special one.

After Sophie had gone back to work, Jamie's mother took him to one side. 'I'm not going to interfere,' she said.

He gave her an arch look. His mother was the epitome of interference.

She noticed, and flapped a hand dismissively. 'I know I've steamrollered you in the past, but I've learned from Sophie that there's a better way of managing you. I just wanted to make sure you know she's a keeper.'

He nodded. 'I know.'

'Good. Then I'll leave you to do something about it.'

Given that he knew Sienna had video calls with both of her grandmothers, he asked, 'I take it Sienna's told you what she wants?'

'She has,' Gwen agreed. 'And Rose and I think that child is wise beyond her years.'

'She is,' Rose said, coming over to them and clearly overhearing the last bit. 'Jamie, you're still a young man. Fran would understand. You're not replacing her—you're opening your life to someone new.'

'Because love doesn't just fit in a box. It grows,' he said.

The grannies looked at each other. 'He's learning,' Gwen said in a stage whisper.

Over the next few days, Jamie found his life changing even more. Somehow he'd agreed to spend Christmas Day with Sophie's parents, Boxing Day with his and New Year's Eve with Fran's.

And Sophie was as warm and sweet when she went out with him and Sienna on a family day as she was when it was just the two of them. Having her back in his life made him realise how much the last two years had been lived in shadows and monochrome. With Sophie, he had the sunshine back and full colour. And it felt *right*.

He thought again about Sienna's request. I want Sophie to be my mummy.

He wanted Sophie, too.

But he needed to show her how special she was to them. How it wasn't going to be like her last two relationships, because this one was for keeps.

In the end, he hatched a plan with Sienna, and invited Sophie over for dinner on Christmas Eve. He made a tagine that could simmer happily without needing any attention; it would take only minutes to steam some green vegetables and cook some couscous. And then he and Sienna spent the afternoon making special shortbread biscuits in the shape of Christmas trees, iced them with melted chocolate, and used sparkly pink sprinkles to spell out each letter of their message.

He just hoped he was doing the right thing.

In every business deal he'd done in the last ten years, he'd known exactly what he was doing. This was fraught with unknowns.

He just had to trust to the wisdom of Santa and the black and white bear.

* * *

'Merry Christmas,' Sophie said when Jamie opened the door to her.

'Merry Christmas.'

'I brought special Christmas chocolates,' she said, handing them to Sienna. 'Reindeers.'

'They're so pretty!' Sienna exclaimed.

Jamie kissed her. 'Come and sit down.'

But when she tried to walk into the kitchen, Jamie ushered her into the dining room instead. 'The kitchen's out of bounds.'

'Because it's a secret,' Sienna said importantly.

Sienna suppressed a grin. Clearly the little girl had helped make dessert and wanted it to be all fanfares and excitement. 'OK.'

Jamie had laid the table in the dining room for the three of them, including crackers, and he'd poured sparkling apple juice for Sienna as well as champagne for Sophie and himself.

'That was fantastic,' Sophie said when she'd finished her tagine. 'I'll help you clear away.'

'No. You have to stay put,' he said.

'If you're sure.' She grinned. 'You make a beautiful waiter, and that little smear of sparkles on the end of your nose is the perfect touch.'

He stared at her, looking shocked. 'I've got sparkles on my face?'

Sienna giggled. 'Pink ones, Daddy. They've been there all afternoon.'

He groaned. 'Sienna, you could've told me.'

'But you always say I look cute with flour on my face,' she pointed out.

'And I think *you* look cute with sparkles on your face,' Sophie added with a grin.

He spread his hands. 'I give in. The sparkles can stay.'

It was a lovely warm family moment that made Sophie want the rest of her days to be like that. But maybe she was being greedy.

Once he'd cleared the table, he returned to announce, 'We have a very special pudding.'

Sienna looked anxious. 'What if we drop it, Daddy?'

'Do you think Sophie should come into the kitchen to see it, instead?' he asked.

She nodded.

'OK. But we don't want to spoil the surprise—Sophie, you have to close your eyes.'

'Don't worry. We'll hold your hand so you won't bump into anything,' Sienna promised.

How could she resist? Sophie closed her eyes and let them take her hands and lead her into the kitchen.

'Stand still and keep your eyes closed,' he said.

She could hear rustling, then a dismayed, 'Daddy, I smudged that one!'

'It's fine, she won't mind,' Jamie reassured Sienna.

'Ta-da!' Sienna said. 'You can open your eyes now.'

She did. And what she saw on the kitchen table was a row of Christmas-tree shaped biscuits, each with a letter made out of sparkly pink sprinkles.

And together they spelled out 'WILL YOU MARRY US?' The 'W' was smudged, as Sienna had said, but it didn't matter. The words blurred as Sophie's eyes filled with tears.

'Sophie?' Jamie asked. 'Are you all right?'

She swallowed hard. 'Yes, just a bit overwhelmed.'

'Will you marry me and make a family with us?' He dropped to one knee. 'The ring's temporary, because if you say yes I thought we could choose the ring together as a family. But for now...' He offered her a small cardboard box that looked as if it was home-made.

She opened it to discover a gold tinsel pipecleaner twisted into the shape of a ring, and felt a single tear spill over her lashes.

'You're crying!' Sienna looked horrified.

'They're happy tears,' Sophie explained, 'not sad ones. Yes, I'll marry you.'

Jamie slid the ring onto the ring finger of her left hand. 'Sorry, it's a little bit too big.'

'We can tweak it.' She twisted it slightly. 'See? Now it's the perfect fit.'

She dropped to her own knees so she was at the same height as Sienna, hugged the little girl and then kissed Jamie.

'So Santa brought me what I really wanted for Christmas after all, even though he said he only gives things you can wrap up,' Sienna said, beaming. 'I knew he would.'

'He brought me what I wanted, too,' Jamie said.

'And me,' Sophie said softly. 'It's going to be a happy, happy Christmas.'

EPILOGUE

Four months later

'I CAN'T BELIEVE that this is Plans & Planes' first wedding abroad—and it's yours!' Eva said, making a last adjustment to Sophie's veil.

'It made sense for our wedding to be the first,' Sophie said with a smile. 'Besides, Iceland's the only place where we're guaranteed a real rainbow in our wedding pictures.'

'And trust you to want a waterfall and rainbows in the background of your wedding pictures,' Eva said, laughing.

'I wanted to have a wedding with a difference,' Sophie said.

'And how.'

There was a knock on the door, and Mandy came in with the two youngest bridesmaids. 'We're done with the hair,' she said with a smile.

'And you two look very beautiful indeed,' Sophie said. Sienna and Hattie were wearing simple white dresses with a ballerina-length tulle skirt and red T-bar shoes. The girls each had a flower crown of red roses, which looked as good in Hattie's straight dark hair as it did in Sienna's mop of blonde curls.

'The rest of the flowers are waiting for you downstairs. A basket of red roses each for the girls, Eva's bouquet of cream roses, and your bouquet of red roses, Sophie,' Mandy said.

'Wonderful. And the corsages and buttonholes?' Sophie asked.

'They're all there, too.' Mandy smiled. 'What with you being a wedding planner and this being your trial run for the new service, everything's running like clockwork.'

'I sorted out all the paperwork early on, talked to the district commissioner and the pastor, and once that's done all the rest is simple. And if there's a brief hitch in the clockwork for any reason,' Sophie said, 'there are back-ups in place.'

'I have the briefcase with all the master plans,' Eva said.

'Which I'll take care of during the service and photographs,' Mandy promised. 'Matt and Angie are keeping an eye on Sam for me, so I can do anything you need me to.'

'Thanks. And I've primed Mum and Gwen to hang onto the capes for the four of us, just in case it gets chilly—even though it's late April,' Sophie said.

'Now, I've made sure Jamie isn't anywhere around to see you before the wedding,' Mandy said. 'I sent him to walk off to the church with Will.' Jamie had asked Sophie's oldest brother to be his best man. 'They're going to text me when they get there.' Her phone beeped and she glanced at the screen. 'And that was your dad to say that the wedding cars will be here in ten minutes.'

'Perfect,' Sophie said. 'And even the weather's being kind to us.' The sun was shining and, because the windows in the hotel were all floor-to-ceiling, the rooms were flooded with light.

'It's going to be a perfect day,' Sienna said. 'The day you marry my daddy and you become my mummy.'

Sophie had to blink back a tear. 'Absolutely, darling.'

Ten minutes later, the three bridesmaids and Sophie's mum were settled in one car, and Sophie went with her father in the other car. It was only a short drive to the church: a beautiful white wooden building with a square tower, a red roof and spire. There were arched windows on the side of the church and the tower, and the square red entrance door had a rose window above it and narrow rectangular windows beside it. From one side, the church was set against the rich green backdrop of the mountainside, counterpointed with the last snow of late spring; on the other, it was set against the rich turquoise of the sea and the dramatic basalt rocks.

'Ready?' Sophie's dad asked.

She nodded.

'For what it's worth, you've definitely picked the right one this time,' he said. 'We all like Jamie very much. And, most importantly, I think he'll make you happy.'

Sophie hugged her father. 'Thanks, Dad.'

The photographer took shots of them in the car and getting out, then in front of the church with the three bridesmaids.

And then it was time to walk down the aisle to Jamie, with the organist playing Bach's 'Jesu, Joy of Man's Desiring'.

Inside, the tiny church was full to bursting with their family and closest friends, crowded into the light wood pews. Everyone was smiling as she walked down the aisle on her father's arm, with Sienna and Hattie behind her and Eva bringing up the rear—but the smile she was focused on was Jamie's, and the way he mouthed 'I love you' as soon as Will had clearly nudged him to let him know that Sophie was walking towards him.

From this day forward...

Sophie took his breath away.

Jamie smiled as his bride walked towards him. Typically Sophie, she'd mixed traditional with a few quirks. She was wearing a simple white dress with an ankle-length tulle skirt, and high heeled red shoes to match the simple bouquet of red roses she carried. Eva's dress was similar but in red, and his daughter and Hattie both looked adorable carrying baskets of roses.

As she reached him at the altar, she mouthed, 'I love you, too.'

The ceremony was as simple and plain as the little church, full of light and love. And when the pastor finally pronounced them married and told Jamie he may kiss the bride, Jamie thoroughly enjoyed flipping Sophie's veil back and kissing her thoroughly.

The organist played Pachelbel's 'Canon' as they signed the register, then switched to Mendelssohn's 'Bridal March' as they walked back down the aisle.

'Well, Mrs Wallis. It's all official now,' Jamie whispered.

She smiled. 'It certainly is.'

The photographer took some group shots outside the church, and then most of the wedding party headed back to the hotel, while Jamie, Sophie, the bridesmaids and Mandy headed out to the Skógafoss waterfall for the final set of photographs.

On the way, it started to rain.

'Don't tell me—your contingency plans involve umbrellas that just happen to match your bouquet?' Jamie teased.

'Funny you should say that,' Sophie teased back. 'Though the saying goes, if you don't like the weather in Iceland, you wait five minutes.'

And, just as they reached the waterfall, the sun came out.

'Perfect timing,' Jamie said.

When the wedding cars had parked, Sophie and Eva both swapped their high heels for flat red pumps so it would be easier to manage the rocky terrain.

'Look, Hattie—there are two rainbows!' Sienna said as they neared the waterfall, and gasped in amazement.

The photographer took the group photographs first, before the little girls got cold enough to need the capes Mandy had brought along. And then the bridesmaids and Mandy headed back to the hotel, leaving the new bride and groom to have the final shots taken.

'This is perfect,' Jamie said, and stole a kiss. 'You look incredible. And with that rainbow... I want one of you on your own, with the waterfall and rainbow behind you, so I can have a framed photo of you on my desk.'

'Great idea. I want one of you, too,' Sophie said.

They were careful not to get so close to the waterfall that Sophie's dress would be soaked by the spray, but the photographer took plenty of shots of her laughing and with her veil blown by the wind as well as more formal poses.

'That's perfect,' the photographer said after a final shot of them together. 'I'll have a file ready for viewing by the time you've eaten, and then I'll come back to do the photographs of the cake-cutting.'

'Thank you,' Jamie said, and shook his hand.

Back at the hotel, everyone was sitting around and talking when they walked in, and a cheer went up.

'I know, I know—you're all starving and we kept you waiting,' Jamie teased. 'But I promise the photographs will be worth it. We got our rainbows.'

He and Sophie stood by the doors to the banqueting suite and welcomed everyone and thanked them for making the trip to Iceland.

'Thank you so much for inviting us,' Rose said when she reached the head of the receiving line. 'I mean, we're not really family...'

'Oh, yes, you are,' Sophie said instantly. 'You're Sienna's grandparents, and that makes you my family.' She hugged the older woman. 'I'm not trying to replace Fran, but I hope you'll come to think of me as family, too.'

Once they'd eaten, Sophie's dad made the first speech. 'Thank you for coming, everyone. The wedding planner told me to keep this very short, and she's a stickler for time management, so short it is.'

Everyone laughed, knowing exactly who the wedding planner was.

'I'm thrilled everyone could make it here to Iceland,' he continued. 'Including my twin grandchildren-to-be.'

Everyone looked at Angie, who simply glowed and patted her bump. 'Thanks to Sophie,' she said.

'I'm hugely proud of my daughter Sophie,' he said. 'She's one of the kindest people I know. And she's going to make an amazing stepmum for my new granddaughter Sienna. I'd like to welcome Jamie and Sienna to the family, and I'd ask you all to raise your glasses to the new Mr and Mrs Wallis. The bride and groom.'

'The bride and groom,' everyone echoed, and clapped as Sophie's father sat down again.

'I too am on a warning from the wedding planner about talking too much,' Jamie said, making everyone laugh. 'I'd like to thank Barney and Jane for welcoming Sienna and me so warmly,' Jamie said. 'And to my parents and Fran's for taking Sophie to their hearts as much as Sienna and I have. I'm thrilled to have married the most gorgeous woman in the world, I'm glad you're all here to share our special day, and I'd like to say a special thank you to Will for being my best man, and to Eva, Sienna and Hattie for being such fabulous bridesmaids. Please raise your glasses to the best man and the bridesmaids— Will, Eva, Sienna and Hattie.'

'Will, Eva, Sienna and Hattie,' everyone chorused.

'I honestly don't know why everyone's so scared of the wedding planner,' Sophie said with a grin. 'All I said was don't rattle on because we want to have cake and dancing. But I'd like to thank everyone for sharing today with us, especially because it meant travelling all this way. And to Aidan's boss for headhunting him—without that, I might never have met Jamie properly.' She smiled. 'And a special thank you to my lovely bridesmaids, all our parents—and I'm including you in that, Rose and Geoffrey—and to Jamie, who let me tear up his ridiculous rule book.'

Everyone laughed, and then Will stood up. 'I'm not scared of the wedding planner at all.' He spread his hands. 'I have video evidence of her singing nursery rhymes to her teddies, seriously out of key, and I'm not afraid to use it.'

'Bring it on,' Sophie called, laughing.

'And because I'm not scared of the wedding planner, we're going to break her timetable and break tradition. Instead of the best man making the speech, it's going to be the youngest bridesmaid.' Will went over to Sienna and lifted her onto her chair, standing by her so she could keep her balance.

'I'm not scared of the wedding planner,' Sienna said. 'Because she's my mummy now and I love her.'

There were audible gulps, and several people had to reach for tissues.

'And me and my best friend Hattie have really pretty dresses,' Sienna continued, undeterred. 'And we saw two rainbows *this* big by the waterfall!' She stretched her arms out wide.

Will whispered in her ear, and she said, 'Oops. Thank you, everyone, for coming. Sophie makes my daddy and me smile again, and I'm glad she's my mummy now. That's all.'

Everyone cheered.

'Well done, kiddo,' Will said, hugging her, then set Sienna back on the floor.

'That's it for the speeches,' Jamie said. 'Cake and dancing, as promised.'

'But because we're getting married in Iceland,' Sophie said, 'we wanted to take one of the Icelandic traditions—the *kransekaka*—so the cake-cutting is going to be a little bit different. How it works is that we cut the first piece, then all the guests come up and break off a piece to eat and make a wish for us.'

She and Jamie posed with a knife in the tiered rings of the conical-shaped cake while the photographer took a few shots, then actually cut the first piece. And everyone came up to break off a piece of cake and wish them every happiness for the future.

Once the cake was done, the singer of the band—who'd been playing quiet guitar and piano music throughout the wedding breakfast—came to the front of the stage. 'We're

Ástrós, and my name's Astrid,' she said. 'We'd like to invite the bride and groom to the floor for the first dance. And we also have guest vocalists—don't we, girls?'

Sienna and Hattie, holding hands, skipped over to the stage.

Jamie looked at Sophie. 'Did you know about this?'

She shook her head. 'Did you?'

He shook his head.

'Mandy,' they said together.

The guitarist played the introduction, and then the girls launched into a slightly off-key version of 'Somewhere Over the Rainbow'. They were a little quiet to start with, and forgot some of the words, but Astrid helped them out and their voices grew stronger and stronger.

'This is the perfect start to our married life,' Jamie said, holding Sophie close and swaying to the music with her.

'A long and happy life,' Sophie said.

'Filled,' Jamie added, 'with rainbows.'

* * * * *